# Blooming Justice

## by

## Peggy Chambers

*Keystone Lake Series*

This is a work of fiction. Names, characters, places, and incidents are either the product of the author's imagination or are used fictitiously, and any resemblance to actual persons living or dead, business establishments, events, or locales, is entirely coincidental.

**Blooming Justice**

COPYRIGHT © 2019 by Peggy Chambers

Cover Art by *Kim Mendoza*

The Wild Rose Press, Inc.
PO Box 708
Adams Basin, NY 14410-0708
Visit us at www.thewildrosepress.com

Publishing History
First Mainstream Mystery Rose Edition, 2019
Print ISBN 978-1-5092-2272-8
Digital ISBN 978-1-5092-2273-5

*Keystone Lake Series*
Published in the United States of America

And just like that his hand was on her butt.

Really? On a first date? Did he really think he'd get that lucky? The laughter from the other table increased—and then it hit her. The date was a show for his friends. She reached down and moved his hand back up. He stepped back ogling her, then pulled her in tighter, grinning and sliding his hand down again. This time, he grabbed a handful of ass as he dipped her backward toward the table. The French twist felt heavy behind her, then the spaghetti strap on the gown popped. She felt her face flush, and he stood her back on her feet.

"Oops," Todd said, leering.

"What are you doing?" She yanked up the borrowed dress, her face burning with embarrassment.

"Just dancin'."

And the music changed to a fast tune.

She stood in shock, facing her date and holding the dress up on one side, her face on fire. Laughter rose around her. She suddenly knew the plan. Get the geek girl to fall for you so you can make fun of her, or worse.

"Need a pin, honey?" Sally Elkman asked with a smirk as she shoved past holding on to the hand of a boy Erin knew only as Train Wreck. Thrusting Erin out of the way, they pushed past leaving her to face her date. Todd grinned as he grabbed her again and twirled her around, then pulled her toward him.

## Praise for Peggy Chambers

"With a solid eye for detail and a keen knack for character development, not unexpected in a veteran author, Peggy Chambers' latest book, *BLOOMING JUSTICE*, is a quick-paced, engaging read."

~*J.B. Hogan, author*

~\*~

"I can't think of any writers who pull me into a story as well as Peggy Chambers. *BLOOMING JUSTICE* is a fast ride through dangerous territory."

~*John T. Biggs, author*

## Dedication

Many thanks go out to
Russell N. Singleton, Attorney at Law,
for his help with the legalities involved
in this work of fiction.

~

And thank you to
the late Patti Sneary Schmook, and family,
for their love and instruction of the intricacies
of hiking the shores of Keystone Lake
when we were young.

## Prologue

Sweat trickled between her breasts as she squatted, hiding from the boy in the convertible. Branches clawed at her long legs—clad only in a short skirt—and scratched without mercy. A tall girl, she luckily wore flats on the date, never knowing she would be on foot tonight. She stood and pushed her matted blonde hair out of her face. In the distance, she could see the rectangular tail lights of the Alpha Romeo convertible as it sped away. The one she couldn't wait to ride in and was now glad to be out of.

The evening had been fun at first. She found him attentive and he took her to a restaurant for dinner that her family could never afford—part of his charm, she had to admit. But the looks, car, money, and charm all rolled into a package made him hard to resist.

After dinner, he showed her the lake. She'd grown up there, but never traveled to that side. The side with all the mansions—places her kind were not normally invited. He knew the backroads, every hill and curve, and he showed her how the car responded to the open road. The top of the convertible down, the wind blew through her hair. Her mother said the golden locks were her best feature and made her resemble a Disney princess. After that, she vowed never to cut it.

He parked the car under a tree where the tree frogs sang, and crickets joined the ensemble. She loved the outdoors and after the ride through the back roads at breakneck speed, she felt alive. She smiled and sank down into the seat staring at the water.

Without warning, he grabbed a handful of that blonde hair and yanked her head backward then pressed his lips to hers cutting them on her teeth. She tasted blood. Ripping her blouse open he grabbed her breast and squeezed hard. The adrenaline still in her system from the car ride helped her when she twisted away.

"No!" she yelled and reached for the door handle.

He pulled her back by her hair. "What do you mean, no? Just a minute ago you were completely up for this!" His ice blue eyes were fierce in the dark.

"Up for what? I loved the car ride but that gave you no right…"

"Bitch, I bought you an expensive dinner. I let you ride in the car. You owe me." He yanked her toward him by her long golden hair.

She doubled her fist and swung. In the tiny car, the punch landed mid chest. It must have surprised him and gave her time to grab the door handle and jump out of the low-slung vehicle. Once out she ran, never even glancing back. Afraid he would come after her, she stumbled into the brush near the water. There were lots of places to hide. Crawling behind a bush she waited to hear if he still searched for her.

The car engine revved once and then again; and she heard the squeal of tires.

## Chapter 1

Erin Sampson received her high school diploma this year, crossing over into adulthood. And the last step in that rite of passage, the senior prom, was always a big deal. Regardless of how many times she told herself otherwise, she knew better. After high school, she planned to live at home and work her way through college and law school at her mother's flower shop. Mom needed her—and she needed the money. Not a girly girl, she knew the value of work and had her feet on the ground.

But the senior prom—a dream come true.

Or maybe a nightmare.

"Why did he ask me at the last minute?" Erin whined.

"Because he's a guy? You know how some boys are." Erin's mother, Alice, tied a bow on a plant.

"I thought I'd never have a chance with Todd of all people. I'd just go with Bernadette if I went at all. And I have nothing to wear."

"Your Aunt Toni has lots of clothes she would loan you. You know she loves to dress you up. She should have had a daughter. If she had, though, she wouldn't be a partner in a law firm, I imagine. She wouldn't be invited to all the social and political affairs. She wouldn't drive a fancy car and have all the things that go with her life." Alice sat the plant aside and tied a second bow to match the first.

Small town Mannford sat on Keystone Lake near Tulsa, Oklahoma. The tiny nook in the giant grocery store that served as the flower shop would be packed with seniors preparing for the prom tomorrow. Today the workers prepared in advance of the onslaught.

"Ask Aunt Toni."

"Do you wish you were her, Mom?" Erin took the first plant and placed it in the delivery box with the others.

"No, babe. I like my life just like it is. I wouldn't change a thing, except still having your dad around. If I could change anything it would be to keep him a little longer and prevent that truck from sliding off the road. But since he's not here, it's just us girls. I have you, and that's enough. You're the one who wants to be like your aunt." Alice smiled at her daughter and placed the last plant in the box.

"Do you think Aunt Toni would loan me the silver strappy one?" Erin saw Aunt Toni in the dress the night she came by the house on the way to an event and fell in love with it.

"I think she would loan you anything you want. Okay, that is the last of the deliveries. Can you get those out for us?"

Erin grabbed the keys to the delivery van and kissed her mother's cheek. "I'll call Aunt Toni on the road."

"Use the speaker on your cell and drive carefully," her mother shouted as Erin ran out the shop door.

Just another day at the flower shop. Erin always came by after school and helped her mother. But tomorrow the school sponsored the prom and Mom and the women at the shop were busier than normal.

\*\*\*\*

Saturday morning, girls jostled for position in line past the potted mums on the floor and wound their way around the cooler filled with flower arrangements. Many of them had shiny, almost plastic hair piled on top of their heads with sparkling jewels. Their hair, in deep contrast to the shorts and t-shirts they wore with dirty flip-flops, a promise of a fairytale evening. The prom scheduled tonight required flowers. Some of the girls prepared for this event for months like a wedding. The hair, nails, and especially the dress, had to be perfect. The guy, not so much. He just matched the dress. Erin wondered if men ever felt like arm-candy at times like this.

"I said the ribbon was to be fuchsia! I gave you a swatch of the fabric, you cow. Now I want fuchsia!" The curls on top of her head bounced each time she slammed the box containing the delicate wristlet down on the counter, the swatch of fabric still attached. The ribbon matched the fuchsia fabric perfectly.

"Sally," crooned the older woman, probably the girl's mother, "don't be rude to the help. I'm sure that is the best she can do. The colors are almost the same. And besides, it will be dark in there."

"It's not what I want." The girl clenched her teeth.

"Let me see if I have something else." Alice took the box off the counter and walked to the back leaving the other women at the counter to deal with the crowd. The cash register rang relentlessly. "Erin, can you help me?" Alice called back over her shoulder, her daughter exiting the walk-in cooler with a load of boxes and tickets in her hands. Erin dropped the boxes and tickets on the counter for the other employees to hand out to the rightful owners, then followed her mother through the bucket-lined path of flowers on the floor to the other end of the shop.

"Can you reach that fuchsia lace all the way at the top?"

A tall girl, Erin reached as far as she could, then grabbed the pole with the hook and stretched again. She snagged the spool of ribbon marked "Fuchsia Dream" and pulled it down.

"This one?"

"Yeah, let's try that one." The iridescent lace matched the swatch of fabric taped to the box and Alice quickly made a small bow. Untying the ribbon on the corsage, she replaced it with the lace one and fluffed the flowers again before snipping and gluing a few extras to replace the ones pulled loose from the untying.

"Why are you doing this?" Erin watched her mother's swift action.

"Because this ribbon doesn't match the dress."

"But they're the same color. This one is just lace. The name is even the same on the label." Erin read the label on the spool of ribbon.

"We know that. Maybe she won't realize. The customer is always right." Alice shrugged her tired shoulders.

"I think it was better the first time."

Alice smiled and walked back where the girl stood tapping her foot as her mother attempted to sooth her mood.

Erin always thought her mother smelled like flowers—carnations—the smell of a flower shop in bloom. The lowly carnations always over-took the scent of all the other flowers in the shop, no matter how elegant they were. The carnations still smelled the best. And when you mixed them with fresh eucalyptus, the scent came directly from heaven. Her mother never needed perfume.

"Try this." Alice handed the box to the customer who just recently berated her so loudly. But the girl refused to take it, her nose in the air pointed the opposite way. After an awkward silence, her mother stepped in and took the box from Alice's outstretched hand and carefully opened it. The mother smiled showing the box to her daughter.

"Look sweetie, it matches perfectly."

Sally took the delicate wristlet out of the box and held it up to the light next to the fabric swatch. She turned it over and viewed it from the backside.

"I suppose it will have to do if it is the best you have." Tossing it back into the box, she stomped off as her mother handed over the credit card with a strained smile. "Next time I'll shop somewhere else." Sally shouted over the crowd of customers.

Sally Elkman. Erin knew her from school. She terrorized the underclassmen on a regular basis. She not only appeared stupid, but colorblind, and had no idea if the ribbon matched the dress or not. Why did people put up with her? But somehow, she climbed over enough bodies to be on top of the pile of social misfits that the school called the elite, and she held court most days at the high school. Next year in college Erin wondered if Sally would fare as well on campus.

"Erin, can you start blowing up balloons? We need twelve bunches of six—each on extra-long ribbons with streamers in the dark pink and purple. Bag them and put them out in the delivery area once they're finished."

Erin shuddered. "You mean fuchsia and plum?"

"You know it." Alice smiled wearily.

The colors of the season were fuchsia and plum, and everyone wore them. Everyone but Erin. She borrowed her aunt's silver gown that touched the floor with strappy sandals to match. Most of the dresses were short enough to be a blouse. But this one had a deep slit up the side that showed muscular legs. The heels were low by some standards, only two inches, but Erin's height made up for them. She couldn't dance in anything any taller. Not that she danced very well. Her plan to dance as little as possible so not to make a fool of herself—still a nugget in her mind.

"Earth to Erin. Balloons?" her mother said, bringing her back to reality.

"Got it. We need a million plum and fuchsia balloons blown up and in the delivery area, stat!"

"Only seventy-two, and as fast as you can do it without hurting yourself. After all, you're the best we have at blowing them up without popping them."

"Great, I'm the balloon queen."

"Well, we've all got to be queen of something." Once more her mother handed out corsages to eager hands.

Erin dug through the organized drawers of her mother's shop and pulled out packages of balloons. Thirty-six pukey-pink balloons. God, fuchsia made her sick. She hoped to never see fuchsia again.

The loud bang and rush of air took her by surprise. The purple balloon blew into a million pieces, the neck still stuck on the tank and goo dripped off Erin's chin. The noise in the shop stopped instantly and all eyes were on the helium tank and the girl operating it. The overused color dripped from the neck of the canister, a ghastly reminder of the season.

Regaining her composure as the conversations began again, Erin tied the balloon bunches together and gathered them into the plastic trash bags corralling them into the delivery area. Cool air blew in the double doors near the loading dock as Sheila pushed in a cart filled with centerpieces for the head table and placed them on the counter.

Chapter 2

"We're never going to get all these in the van at the same time." Sheila spoke to Erin as she lifted the bouquets out of the cart. "What time are you leaving to get ready?"

"About thirty minutes ago." Erin placed a weight on the balloon streamers to keep them from floating away.

"You have your dress with you?"

"Yes, but I planned to rush home and get a shower. Felicity was going to do my hair. Now, I'm beginning to wonder if I'll ever get out of here."

"You'll just have to leave, and we'll take care of it. Here, you still have goo on your chin. Either that or you are growing white whiskers." Sheila giggled and wiped Erin's chin. She served as the shop's assistant manager even though paid like everyone else—minimum wage. Her mother's salary, paid by the big corporate superstore, probably paid her less than her workers, if you added her hours together.

"All right girl, get out here and be ready to be beautiful!" Felicity's short blond hair had a pink stripe today and poked through the door of the delivery area. Her green eyes sparkled as she surveyed the room. "Good Lord, could we get some more pink and purple? It's like a giant bubble gum dispenser in here. Who picked out these colors? Not your mom."

"No, not Mom. But as she always says, 'the customer is always right'—or maybe wrong."

"Well when are you going to be done? What time is the date picking you up?"

"Date! Crap! I almost forgot. I need to text Todd and tell him to just meet me there." Erin pulled the phone from her back pocket and sent her first-time date the bad news that she might be late. She wondered how he would take it.

"Well, put down the balloons and get in the bathroom. Clean up a little and I'll do your hair when you get done." Felicity, not her mother, sometimes filled that part. When she made up her mind that Erin should do something, Erin just went along.

"She's right," Sheila chimed in. "Go get ready for the prom, we'll do the rest." She pushed Erin toward the back room where the unisex employee bathroom sat in the warehouse.

"Now I want you to wash your face, and other unmentionable places that need attention, and I'll take care of your hair and makeup. The dress is in the car, right?" Felicity smiled as she shoved Erin down the hall. A giant bag hung on Felicity's shoulder and Erin wondered what she meant by fixing her up for prom night. You couldn't argue with a person who had pink hair.

"Felicity, it's almost time to close. Surely I can help Mom with the last of the pick-ups and then load the van."

"Sheila and your mom will finish up and load the van. Go get ready!"

Erin walked into the oversized square bathroom. Unisex and handicap accessible. The corporation spared no expense. One bathroom shared by fifty plus employees. At least it smelled clean.

Her long dark hair in a pony-tail, she scrubbed her face with the liquid soap for hands. Then she pulled off the T-shirt and used a wet paper towel under her arms. Why did she not remember deodorant?

Pulling off her jeans she stood in sock feet on the cool tiled floor. With prom and graduation week, laundry sat undone. She wore the pink sparkly panties she received in a package last Christmas. At least they didn't have the days of the week written on them. They served their purpose. No one would see them anyway, but she hoped they wouldn't show through the silver dress. She tugged the panties off and cleaned as well as she could with a wet paper towel and then dressed again.

"Are you decent?" Felicity called from outside the door. "Wet your hair while you're in there and I'll blow it dry."

"I just want a French twist, nothing fancy."

"Of course, it just needs a little height."

"Only a little," Erin mumbled under her breath. She knew how crazy hair stylists got when they started sometimes.

Erin emerged from the bathroom and found a line waiting to get in. Haggard employees stood waiting their turn with bored expressions on their faces and at the same time in a hurry.

"Sorry," Erin mumbled under her breath.

Felicity tossed Erin a towel for her hair.

"Now, a French twist, huh? How Audrey Hepburn. A little *Breakfast at Tiffany's*?" Felicity smiled.

"It is a simple dress and I think a simple hair style

goes with it."

"I think you could be right. By the way, I thought you might need this." Felicity tossed her a stick of deodorant. Thank God for friends.

Felicity leaned Erin's head forward and began drying the long brown hair. She dried, fluffed, dried again, sprayed, and then dried again. She reached into her bag for pins. "Here, hold this." Felicity handed a box of hair pens for Erin to hold—then finished in an instant. Erin felt the tug of her hair as Felicity pinned it up the back of her head and then the fog of hairspray, that lasted forever, enveloped her. Dried for a second—then more hairspray.

"Beautiful hair, so thick and shiny most women would kill for this. I guess that is what you get for being eighteen." Felicity sighed. She took the box of pins from Erin and picked up the makeup kit lying in the monstrous bag on the floor. She sat the kit on Erin's lap, pulled out a huge powder brush with loose powder and swept it across her face.

"Just a little, I don't want to resemble a hooker." Felicity hushed her with a lip brush to her lips for color, and then applied lip gloss.

"Just a little is all you need. Now hold still for some mascara and don't you dare let those eyes water!"

"There. Not so awful huh? Now check out the mirror and see what you think."

"You're done already?" Erin said in surprise, gingerly touching her hair.

"Well, you're late, I had to hurry. Now go!"

Erin walked in the bathroom, which now smelled like five people used it, and stepped in front of the dimly lit mirror over the sink. Her olive skin was amazing. Felicity handed her a mirror. "Here, you can see the back."

Erin twisted around with the mirror in her hands to view the back of her hair. Just like Erin would have done it herself—if she had the time and talent.

"You look great, honey." Alice stood in the doorway. "Run get your dress. I want to see the whole package."

"Alice." Sheila walked to the door glancing at her watch. "There's no way the balloons and flowers will all fit in the van and make it to the school in one trip, and we're already running late."

"Put the excess in the Honda." Erin reached in her pocket pulling out the keys to the car. The ageing vehicle took her back and forth to school and work for the last two years. Reliable most of the time, and if not, she hitched a ride with Bernadette.

"No. You have to get dressed." Alice handed the keys back.

"I'll get dressed after I get there, just pack it up. I'll help you unload first. It's almost time!"

The prom committee stood wringing their hands when the delivery van pulled up. Erin, her mother and Sheila placed flowers on the head table and then tied the balloons on the legs of the tables. Erin ignored the committee's complaints as she worked.

"You're late," Sally snapped at Alice.

"I'm sorry. We had a lot to do and not enough help to do it. But this place is amazing, don't you think?" Alice surveyed the room.

"There's too much fuchsia. I guess you ran out of plum? I suppose it will have to do." Sally stood with her hands on her hips.

Erin rolled her eyes at her classmate, then stepped back—her eyes were drawn to the dance floor as the mirror ball began to turn. She shrugged Sally's attitude off and walked away deciding the confrontation was not worth it.

"Okay, ladies let's get out of here." Alice herded the florists out the door to the van. Erin followed, and at the van she kissed her mother goodbye.

"Bye, Mom, I promise to be home early!" Erin thought of Cinderella in reverse, as she ran for the car, avoiding anyone she knew—hopeful her hair held up.

The Honda, parked at the end of the parking lot in a dark corner where she left it after unloading, held her prom clothes. She climbed in the back seat. Pulling her arms out of the T-shirt, she changed into the strapless bra she borrowed with the dress, then kicked off her tennis shoes and socks. The shimmery dress slipped over her head, then she pulled the T-shirt off, careful of her hair. Somehow, she managed to get on her knees in the compact seat and pulled the zipper tab up the back of the dress—then wriggled out of the jeans still underneath.

The shoe box lay in the floorboard of the car and she kicked off its top as moonlight shone in the windows and bounced off the silver pedicure her mother and Felicity gave her last night. Silver toenails matched the dress perfectly.

Fully dressed, she flipped on the dome light and checked her makeup. The French twist still held up even after all the deliveries. She shook her head slowly from side to side and it never moved. The hairspray might remain after several washings. Reaching in the makeup bag she replaced the lip gloss eaten off as she worked, then put it in her evening bag as Felicity suggested. She doubted she would remember to use it again. The only other things in the silver bag were her cell phone and keys. Long dangly earrings with clear stones set in silver hung from her ear lobes, and with a quick spritz of the perfume she borrowed from her mother, she glanced at her watch and realized the time—then she saw the ragged nails. She always chewed them when stress hit, and it came down in buckets lately. The fake ones were still in the bag—silver like the dress.

A drop of glue on each finger, she pressed the nails to her fingertips and slowly counted to sixty. Another minute wouldn't matter. Hopefully they would remain in place all night and not flip across the room into someone's drink.

Fully dressed, Erin took a deep breath and stepped out of the aging car. She walked across the parking lot into the starry night to meet the boy she thought she would never have a chance with.

## Chapter 3

Todd lay across the bed propped up on pillows in his tennis shorts. Sweat trickled down his chest and pooled in his navel. He really needed to shower, but for now he would stay in his room to avoid Dad. He played poorly today and there would be hell to pay. Dad didn't like losing, but more than that, he didn't like losers. That's what Dad thought of his son. He considered him a loser. The ceiling fan, swirled a light breeze through the open windows down and across his sweaty body, lulling him into a drowsy state.

His father set up the match last week with Judge Hardridge and his son, Jake. Doubles was never Todd's game, especially with Dad. He played better alone. But his father insisted. Todd knew the judge and his son well. Jake, a year older and already in college, grew up with Todd at the country club. Jake, okay in a geeky kind of way, displayed a mean backhand if you were unprepared. Something you didn't expect from a computer nerd if you didn't know him. Todd learned to watch out for that backhand. What Todd hadn't expected was the short spike just barely over the net that won the game. And he would pay for that mistake.

Todd jolted awake as the door banged open and bounced off the wall behind. He sat up quickly. His father stomped in the room, scotch sloshing in the glass. Todd could smell the woody odor of alcohol wafting off him from across the room.

"You're a loser. And what's worse, you made me look like a loser out there today too." He slurred his words staring angrily at his teenaged son.

"Dad it's not my fault. Who knew the little squirrel could play?"

"You should have known! You grew up with him on the tennis courts!"

"I knew he had a mean backhand sometimes, but the spike took me by surprise."

"Surprise? Well, I'm surprised that you even showed up today. You played as if you were somewhere else. I've seen you play better when you were twelve." Todd's father shook his head and took a long draw on the drink staring down his nose at his son.

Todd's older brother, out of the house these days, left Todd to deal with Dad on his own. With Paul away at college, Dad had only one son to rebuke, and he did it in fine form.

Paul stood up for Todd many times when they were kids and took the rap when he shouldn't have—like the day Todd scratched Dad's new Mercedes dropping the bike in a hurry. An A on his history exam needed to be shared and he wanted to show it to someone—anyone—especially Dad. As a child he still had some respect for the old man. It took a while to learn he would never be good enough for him. Todd dropped his bike in a rush and it scratched his dad's new car. When the inevitable fight broke out and punishment handed down, Paul stepped in and said he scratched it, to protect his little brother. He then spent a month grounded from all electronic devices, after withstanding his father's wrath. Every night of that month, Todd would sneak into his brother's room allowing him to borrow his iPad as his father snored just down the hall. The brothers had always been close. They had to be just to survive a tyrannical father and mousy mother afraid of her own shadow.

Mom would do nothing. Dad scared her too and she'd never stand up against him. Not for anyone, not even for her own kids. Wasn't a mother supposed to protect her young? Even in the wild, bears and tigers did that. But his mother wasn't a bear or a tiger. He thought of her as more of a mouse. Women! The older he got, Todd started hating his mother. His father, however, he'd hated for a long time.

"Your mom is waiting for you, so she can have Lucinda serve dinner. Get down there, but not before you shower the stink of defeat off and change your clothes. And hurry up!" He stomped out the door leaving it standing open and grumbling as he descended the stairs. Todd kept thinking someday in a drunken stupor Dad would fall headlong down those stairs and maybe break his neck. No one would mourn him. But so far, Todd wasn't that lucky. His father seemed to be able to keep his feet under him and the scotch in the glass. Just like he managed business deals during the day. The world didn't know the man he showed his family at night where he was a dictator in his own home, but his family did.

Dad was right about one thing, Todd needed a shower. But, he would always stink to his Dad no matter how clean he presented himself. However, tonight he didn't want to deal with it. He had other plans.

The senior prom—not any big deal—provided him

with a new girl. Someone he'd not gone out with before, and he had plans for her. He'd show her a good time.

He headed for the shower, his tux hung behind the door.

His hair still damp, he crept down the stairs, avoiding the living room where his parents awaited his arrival, and out the back door.

His Alpha Romeo shimmered in the moonlight, and he jumped in the driver's seat. Todd revved the engine once listening to the purr. It might have been the only thing in life he'd loved in a long time. Its sleek lines responded to his touch like no other and he raced down the street to the gymnasium where the school held the final prom of his life.

Dinner could wait forever.

## Chapter 4

The mirror ball gave a surreal appearance to the gym garbed in shadows and light. Erin stopped before entering the room and gazed around. There was a fluffy orange ball bouncing her way. Only petite Bernadette could pull off a style like that. She wore a short and almost neon-orange dress, with layers of tulle skirt like a tutu. Strapless over her ample bust, except for a piece of netting pulled across one shoulder, it held up the entire creation. At the top of her shoulder sat a rose made of the same fabric that tied it all together. Her curly brown hair loose around her shoulders, she sported pink ballet slippers on her feet. Her Cleopatra styled eyeliner accentuated green eyes. Black and white nail polish shone on her nails decorated with cartoon characters and Erin knew she'd hand painted them. Bernadette spent hours rummaging through second hand stores or made the dress herself. She didn't buy off the rack.

"OMG! Your dress is great!" Bernadette stared her best friend up and down. "Have you seen Todd yet? "

"No, I just got here. Yours is cute too! Where did you get it? And your nails are darling! I hate that I'm late, but you know the shop—busy today, and I just couldn't leave." Erin pulled her strap back up and in place, aware of her nervous talking.

"No, I haven't seen him yet." Both girls scanned

the room at the last prom of their school years.

"Are Steve and Rob here?" Erin knew her best friends were coming to the prom together tonight. She would have been with them if she hadn't been invited by Todd.

"Yeah, they're over there somewhere. Oh, here comes Todd!" Bernadette squealed. "Have a good time and dance a little so I can get pictures." Bernadette flitted away like a fairy in an orange grove on her pale pink slippers.

"You look wonderful tonight." Todd spoke walking up beside her. She thought she saw the flash of a camera behind her as they walked away. "What a lovely dress." His amazing smile and perfect teeth lit up the room. The clear, ice blue eyes that Erin thought she would never see up close, flashed in the shadows brought on by dim light. He leaned in and lightly kissed her on the cheek and took her hand leading her to the tables.

"I'm sorry to be late, the shop was crazy with all the orders," she said stammering for something to say.

"Are you hungry? I'm starving." He ignored her rambling and handed her a plate from the appetizer table.

Over in the corner stood a table by itself where no one sat. Todd nodded to the table, and she followed his lead walking beside him.

Passing the group of jocks and their dates she heard snickers. Did athletes make fun of everything? Were they just socially inept, or did they really think everything funny—like the geek girl hanging out with the team captain. She was still confused about why he invited her tonight, and the thought made her uncomfortable. Something didn't feel right.

"Want to sit here?" Todd asked gesturing.

She glanced up at the balloons again and noticed one losing its helium and sagging. It had a hole that the liquid latex didn't fill. Then she stopped herself from thinking about work at the senior prom. This was her night and she needed to enjoy it.

"You look wonderful tonight," he said again. Smiling, he lifted his fork to his mouth.

"Thank you," she murmured. Having trouble holding her gaze in those blue eyes, Erin smiled and then looked over his shoulder. She saw Rob on the other side of the room staring at her. He nodded, and she nodded back.

Todd glanced across the room at the table full of his friends and snickered. They were beginning to make a lot of noise. Did he want to be with them?

He turned back to Erin, "Wanna' dance?"

"Um, yeah, I guess. But I must warn you, I haven't had much practice." She began to sweat just thinking of dancing. They walked in the direction of the noisy table and he pulled her close.

And just like that his hand was on her butt.

Really? On a first date? Did he really think he'd get that lucky? The laughter from the other table increased—and then it hit her. The date was a show for his friends. She reached down and moved his hand back up. He stepped back, ogling her, then pulled her in tighter, grinning and sliding his hand down again. This time, he grabbed a handful of ass as he dipped her backward toward the table. The French twist felt heavy behind her, then the spaghetti strap on the gown popped. She felt her face flush, and he stood her back on her feet.

"Oops," Todd said, leering.

"What are you doing?" She yanked up the borrowed dress, her face burning with embarrassment.

"Just dancin'."

And the music changed to a fast tune.

She stood in shock, facing her date and holding the dress up on one side, her face on fire. Laughter rose around her. She suddenly knew the plan. Get the geek girl to fall for you so you can make fun of her, or worse.

"Need a pin, honey?" Sally Elkman asked with a smirk as she shoved past holding on to the hand of a boy Erin knew only as Train Wreck. Thrusting Erin out of the way, they pushed past leaving her to face her date. Todd grinned as he grabbed her again and twirled her around, then pulled her toward him.

"Let's get out of here," he said suggestively.

Stunned, Erin steamed in anger. Really, did he think he could get away with that behavior? "Not with you!" She yanked up her dress and turned to leave. He grabbed her hand and pulled her back into him, nuzzling her neck.

"Aw come on, honey, don't be like that." He ran his hands down her backside again and she reacted the only way she knew. She raised her knee as hard as she could, catching him square in the groin and ripping the slit in the evening gown even higher, showing a hint of bright pink panties underneath. When he folded in front of her she almost missed the blur that rushed in and helped him stand back up with an uppercut to the jaw. It knocked him over and onto the table full of jocks and their dates, cake and punch flying. And just like that, her three best friends were there to save her. Rob jumped on top of Todd in an instant with Bernadette and Steve right behind him.

What happened next in the whirlwind of students yelling, people running, and lastly Coach and the English teacher pulling the guys apart, Erin never saw. She stared at the melee, spun on her heels, and left the gym she helped decorate, for the solitude of the warm night air.

Always her knight in shining armor, Erin heard Rob running behind her calling her name as she crossed the parking lot to the dark corner that held her car. He caught up to her and she saw the shiner he sported. Proof that Todd must have gotten in at least one good punch.

"Are you okay?" He studied her with genuine concern.

"I'm fine. Just humiliated and wearing a borrowed dress that won't be returned in as good of shape as I received it."

"Newman should pay for that."

"I don't want to ask him for anything. I stupidly went out with him in the first place."

Her hands were shaking badly when she attempted to unlock the door of her car trying not to cry in front of Rob.

"Here let me." Rob took the keys from her and opened the door. "I'll drive."

She found she didn't care, relieved to let someone else take care of things for once.

The drive home deathly quiet, Erin resolved not to let Rob see her cry. She knew for some time that Rob cared for her as more than just a friend. But she told him she didn't want a relationship. College and a degree were at the top of her list and couldn't afford the distraction. And then she made a fool out of herself with prince charming tonight. She should know better.

"Thank you for helping me out tonight," Erin said stepping out of the car. She straightened her dress and stood tall before walking to the door.

"Anytime." He smiled and walked away. Later she wondered how he got home.

## Chapter 5

"There's the queen of the hop!" Aunt Toni spoke over the top of a blue margarita glass.

"Queen of the Hop? Aunt Toni how old are you?" Erin walked into the kitchen she grew up in wearing the damaged, borrowed, dress. Her mother and aunt sat at the table as they often did on the weekend around a pitcher of margaritas. Felicity sometimes joined them and even spent the night—just to be safe.

"Honey, what happened to the dress?" Erin's mom stood as she walked in.

Erin, determined not to let her mother know about the prom disaster, composed herself after Rob left her at the door.

"Just a little accident on the dance floor, Mom." She held the dress up on the side with the broken strap. "Bernadette says her mom can fix it. I'm going to take it to her in the morning." The room sat silent. Erin eyed the woman she borrowed the silver gown from. "Really, Aunt Toni, the dress will be okay."

"I'm sure it's fine," her aunt waved the problem off like nothing. "But why are you home so early?" Aunt Toni examined the slit in the dress from across the table.

"Oh, just tired. I think I'll go to bed as soon as I shower all this hair spray out."

Silence again. Erin, terrified there might be more

questions, quickly turned to go to her room.

"Well, hang on a second." Mom walked around the kitchen table and put her hand on Erin's shoulder. "We never expected you so early from your senior prom. But your aunt has something to ask you." Erin froze.

Aunt Toni glanced up with a twinkle in her eye as Erin held the dress together with one hand. "How would you like to go to work for Cronkite and Associates as a law clerk this summer?"

Erin paused. Then this wasn't about the dress? "What? I have a job at the flower shop with Mom." Relieved that there was no more grilling about the prom, the question began to sink in and her eyes were wide in shock. A law office?

"Well this is a better one." Aunt Toni smiled and sipped her drink. "It is a great opportunity for you to see if law is really what you want and is good for the firm. We can use and abuse you full time in the summer, and then part time in the fall when you go back to school. And there will be a little money in it for you."

Erin turned back to her mother, who nodded. The dress and Todd forgotten for the moment.

Erin thought she would work for her mother until she graduated. She needed a part time job in college. But this…

"I don't know what to say." Erin glanced at her aunt and then back at her mother who radiated pride at her only child.

"Well, then say yes," Mom said.

"But who will help you?"

"Sheila's daughter needs a job. I've already talked to her," Alice replied.

"Can she blow up balloons?" Erin always took care of balloons at the shop. She had a knack for seeing just how tight they were getting before they broke. Most of the time.

"We'll teach her." Alice reached for a chip and dipped it in salsa.

Erin thought for moment. Could she be replaced that easily? After all it didn't take a Rhodes Scholar to learn to blow up a balloon. Of course, someone else could do it. And the reality of the offer set in. She would be working at a law office like her aunt.

"Well then yes!" Erin squealed with delight and hugged her aunt. "A law firm! When do I start?"

"How's Monday?" her aunt asked raising on eyebrow.

Erin, determined to attend college in Tulsa even with little money, had a scholarship, a job, and could live at home. It might not be the glamorous way to go to college, but it worked for her. The University of Tulsa had a law school on campus once she received her undergraduate degree. As a National Merit finalist, her grades were good enough to get her into TU and give her the scholarship money she needed. Besides, if she lived at home until she graduated, Mom wouldn't be alone, and she could help at the flower shop now and then. She hoped to be able to CLEP out of most of the freshman basics, so she could advance quickly. TU also had a program for pre-law and she could finish her bachelors in three, instead of four years, if she passed the LSAT test. If, if, if...

After hugs all around the table, Erin excused herself to shower. She could still hear her mother and aunt in the kitchen as she put on her pajamas and sank into the bed she'd slept on most of her life. The incident at the prom forgotten for the moment she lay staring up at the ceiling—she would be working in a law firm come Monday morning. What a great opportunity.

The only one of the four friends who would not live on campus, Erin could still see them when there. The four would still be together.

TU would be great—except for the fact that Todd would be there also.

Chapter 6

Dressed in the skirt and flats that Erin and her mom picked out the night before, she climbed into the car—its doors creaked so loudly, even the neighbor's sleepy basset hound opened his eyes. Rob helped clean the car yesterday after they made a trip into the city to find the law office. The aging leather seats were slick with conditioner, and she'd found her study notes from history class last spring, still under the seat. There were cups and wrappers from drive-through trips and general grime, enough to fill a kitchen trash bag. Rob suggested maybe with all her hard work, she should think about her car now and then too and promised to grease the door hinges for her soon. She knew it needed attention—not just gasoline—but it worked hard for her. Just what she needed going back and forth to school and work. But like the skirt, she needed to present a more professional appearance now. She stepped up in the world from a high school girl in a flower shop, to a college woman working in a law firm.

Pulling into a parking place meant for visitors, she stepped out of the car and walked to the door of the distinguished brick building and took a deep breath. The warm moist air made her sweat. She brushed her hair away from her face.

"You can do this Erin Elaine Sampson." She spoke to herself in her mother's tone, the voice that always gave her courage. The praise helped Erin in times of doubt. The prom and high school behind her, now she could move on. She smiled her best smile and pulled the door open with a yank—only to come face to face with an older man in glasses, white slicked-back hair, and a brief case in his hand.

"Deliveries are in the back." He grumbled ambling past her. She could smell cigar smoke and a faint scent of familiar cologne.

"I'm not delivering anything. I'm supposed to start work this morning." Erin knew her answer sounded immature.

He turned scrutinizing her up and down, then sighed. "They're making them younger and younger." He shook his head and walked away from her grumbling under his breath.

Ignoring the comment, she mounted the stairs that appeared to go forever. Rounding the corner for the second half of the staircase she could see the glass door at the top. "Cronkite and Associates" it read in bold black letters outlined in gold. She pushed the door open, stepped into the oak paneled waiting room, and walked to the receptionist sitting primly behind the desk. She barely glanced up at Erin. So much for customer service.

Erin cleared her throat. "I'm Erin Sampson. I'm supposed to start work this morning."

"You're late." The receptionist slowly raised her head.

"It's a quarter of eight. I'm supposed to be here at eight o'clock."

"Like I said, you're late." The tall, thin woman with long dark hair stood and gestured for Erin to follow her. She walked ahead in platform heels and straight skirt. "Talk to Sara about the forms you need to fill out, and then she will show you were to sit." The receptionist turned on her heel, the phone ringing, she punched the button on the earpiece as she walked back to her desk leaving Erin standing at the closed door that read "Sara Randolph, Office Manager." Erin knocked.

"Come in." The pleasant voice on the other side of the door a welcome relief to what she had encountered so far.

Opening the door, Erin found a plump older woman sitting behind the desk in a cluttered office. She rose to take Erin's hand. "You must be Erin. Toni has told me so much about you. She is very proud of you, you know? She tells me you are all of eighteen and just graduated high school."

"Aunt Toni is great, but she might exaggerate a little sometimes. Anyway, I'll be nineteen next month."

"Well, happy birthday a little early. By the way around here, she is just Toni or Ms. Stone. You might want to leave off the aunt part, you know how people can be about your aunt hiring her niece. Come with me to one of the conference rooms and we'll get started on your intake paperwork."

Erin followed the woman down halls bustling with activity. Opened doors revealed people behind desks deep in thought staring at computer screens or on the phone in loud argumentative conversations. Erin wondered if she should leave a trail of breadcrumbs to get back to the starting point. The offices formed a square and she was led down the corridor always turning left at the corner. They would probably come back to the beginning if she continued. One man on a cell phone slammed the door shut in their faces when Erin stared as they walked by.

"First time in a law office?" Sara smiled warmly. "You'll get used to it. Remember that their bark is worse than their bite. Here we are. Have a seat and please fill out the forms. Can I get you something to drink?"

"No, I'm fine, thanks." Erin had no idea where to begin on the mountain of paperwork in front of her.

"Did you bring two forms of ID? I don't know if Toni told you, but you'll need to prove that you are a US citizen or legal to work here."

"I have my driver's license, will that work?"

"Here just read the I-9. It tells you what documents are required. You can bring them with you tomorrow. When you're finished, I need you to view some videos about harassment in the workplace and a few others. Just the standard stuff. You'll be here most of the morning. Dial 400 on the phone to reach me if you have any questions and let me know when you will be ready for the videos."

The woman stepped quickly from the room closing the door behind her leaving Erin with a sinking feeling. What had she gotten herself into? Her only other job didn't require all this paperwork. Maybe Mom filled it out for her. She sighed, picked up the pen, and began to write.

"Well, anyway, the old goat slammed the gavel down and yelled 'Order!', like that was going to fix things!"

The door flew open and an attractive man in a dark suit with people behind him stood in the doorway. He appeared surprised to see her.

"You can't be in here, honey, we have a deposition. Go on, get your stuff and scoot."

"Um, Sara put me in here to fill out these forms. I'm Erin by the way." Erin stood with the pen in her hand.

"Well, I'm sorry, but Sara should know we have depositions today. You gotta go." He gestured with his thumb behind him.

A young woman in a business suit slipped past the man and began to place documents on the board table as Erin gathered her things. Her face burning, Erin walked through the door and turned left, hopefully back the way she came, down the corridors toward Sara's office and the front of the building. With no windows in the paneled hallways, she could only guess which way she came in.

"Well, she knew better when she committed the offense. What can I say?" A familiar voice. Aunt Toni sat in her office with red stilettos propped up on the desk talking on the phone.

Erin lightly rapped on the door facing and Toni glanced up. She instantly changed from business to family and smiled.

"Okay, gotta go. Just get the continuance and we'll reschedule." She hung up the phone.

"Erin! So good to see you. I assumed Sara had you hoppin' already. I was gonna' check on you a little later this morning."

"Well, Sara set me up in a board room filling all this out, and a man told me to leave because he had a deposition. He said she should have known when she put me there."

"Who sent you packin'?" Toni took her feet down

and sat up in the leather chair.

"I have no idea."

"Have a seat. We'll get to the bottom of this." Erin sat down in the chair across from the desk and viewed the beautifully furnished room. It held cherry bookcases and desk to match. Not that she knew anything about rugs, but the one on the floor appeared Persian or a good fake. The art, obviously original, and diplomas beautifully framed to match the furniture.

"Sara, Toni. I have Erin in my office and she says she was rousted out of the board room by someone. She doesn't know who. What did he look like, honey?" She covered the phone and spoke to Erin.

"I don't know, young like you, with brown hair and wearing a dark suit. That's about the best I can do."

"Sara, it sounds like Nathan. Did he have a deposition this morning? Okay, let me know. She can just stay here for the moment."

"I'm sorry, Aunt Toni, I didn't mean to cause trouble." Erin adjusted the mountain of paperwork in her lap.

"You didn't cause trouble. It sounds to me like Nathan Williams. He is always acting like the whole place belongs to him and everyone should do his bidding. I need to introduce you to him, but first I'm going to warn you. He can be a real character. Don't let him get under your skin. He's a piece of work when he sets his mind to it. He's sure he is the most important person around here. But for now, just sit here and finish your paperwork. Sara will find out what is going on and put a stop to it. You don't want to mess with Miss Sara. She is tougher than you might think. Just bring your stuff over here to the conference table and work on it. I have some research to do and if you have any questions, don't hesitate to ask."

Erin worked into the morning on the paperwork as Toni researched on the computer when the phone buzzed. Toni spoke quickly and then turned to Erin. "Hon, Stephanie has a job for you."

"Who's Stephanie?" Erin raised her head.

"The receptionist. I assumed you met her on the way in."

"Okay we met. I just didn't get her name."

"Leave the paperwork, you can finish it later. I think she needs some exhibits copied. Turn left when you go out the door and keep going. You'll run right into her desk." Toni returned to the computer screen leaving Erin to find her way back.

****

"Okay, here are the stickers and in here is the copy machine. Nathan needs three copies of each ASAP."

Erin struggled with the pile of papers thrust into her hands. The documents were at least twelve inches thick with a pile of peel-off stickers on the top.

"Okay, let's hustle! You've made copies of exhibits before, right?" Stephanie stood with nail file in hand and one hip thrust out in frustration.

"No. But, I can follow directions."

Stephanie sighed loudly. "Okay, the sticker goes on the bottom right of the top document, and then copy them. Make sure they are all stapled in the exact order and then paper clipped together by document with the original on the top." She spoke so quickly that Erin wished she could take notes.

Stephanie punched the button on the earpiece "Cronkite and Associates," she crooned into the receiver as she walked back to her desk.

The copier was much larger than the one at the store or any she had used in school. The touch-screen display could have been the cockpit of a jet aircraft. She glanced around the room—another conference room, though much smaller than the first one—and placed the documents on the table. In the center of the table sat a station with paperclips, staplers, and other office supplies. She picked up the sheet of stickers marked Plaintiff's Exhibit No. Should she leave it blank? Stephanie said to put them in the lower right-hand corner of each document. A rap on the door and Erin turned to see Sara standing there smiling.

"Just got here and they've thrown you into the lion's den, huh? Let me see if I can help you out." She took the pile of documents from Erin's hands. "Okay, Nathan represents the Plaintiff in this case. See the name at the top? Each of these sets of documents gets a sticker so he can offer them as evidence in court. But he'll need several copies to distribute to opposing counsel, the judge, and one to keep for himself." She laid out the documents in a line as she spoke pulling the staples from each. "Go ahead and put the stickers on the first page and I'll get you started."

The copier, not as daunting as it first appeared, would staple the pages as it went. Originals were going in and copies were coming out in a nice neat line all stapled together—when it stopped dead in its tracks. No more paper came out. Neither the originals nor the copies—and lights were flashing all over the screen. Following the directions on the machine, Erin squatted down on her knees opening doors and reaching into dark recesses feeling for paperwork, when she heard the door open.

"How's it going in here?" Nathan stood outside the door with a briefcase in hand, his slim assistant behind him.

"Um, well. I was almost finished, but the final exhibit is lost somewhere in the copier."

Nathan rolled his eyes. "Janice, help her out." He stepped out and disappeared around the corner.

"Hi, I'm Janice and you're?"

"Erin."

"Okay Erin, first time in a law office?" Janice knelt next to Erin.

"Is it that obvious? Then yes. Sara helped me, and things were going fine until this." She gestured to the machine, trying to keep her voice from sounding whiney.

"Yes, it eats things sometimes. But, Nathan is due in court and needs these exhibits. Let me see what you've got and what needs to be done." She glanced at the stacks of documents with stickers. "Of course, it ate the most important one. Never fails. But, I have another on my desk and there's a second copier down the hall. I'll call I.T. to take care of Jaws here. Bring the stack with you and we'll take them to him at the hearing once we're finished."

The courthouse, a short walk from the brick building occupied by Cronkite and Associates, would be a trip Erin made often. She found a box lid for the exhibits and ran to keep up with Janice, the lid under her arm. The wind threatened to rip the papers from her hands as Erin mounted the steps of the building. Once through the metal detector and security, she followed Janice at a close clip as the woman maneuvered the halls of the seven-story building in heels faster than Erin could keep up in flats.

"All the courtrooms are on the upper floors, four to each floor." Janice exited the elevator and walked quietly down the hall.

Her hair in her face and beads of sweat under her arms, Erin walked in the door held open by the assistant. Inside, the small courtroom appeared to be nothing like Erin expected.

The judge sat behind the bench. The two tables in the front held the attorneys and their clients. Janice quickly took the documents from Erin and walked quietly to the front leaving Erin in the back next to the door. She caught her boss's eye and placed the clipped documents into the folders labeled for each on his table, and then turned and signaled Erin. Time to leave. Her movements were almost imperceptible in the quiet room. Nathan noticed her, but no one else.

Taking the elevator down, Janice spoke, pointing. "The court clerk's office and the county clerk's are both located on the lower floors. You will go there to file documents. I can show you later. And by the way, there is a briefcase at the receptionist's office meant for carrying documents to the courthouse so they don't get damaged on the way. Not that a box lid doesn't work. I found it inventive."

"It's stupid, I know, but it was all I could find in a hurry." Erin felt her face warm once more with embarrassment.

"Don't worry about it. You got them there. That's what counts. I'll give you a copy of a sheet I have with judges' names and their bailiffs, so you can get acquainted when you go over. Sometimes you will need to have an Order signed by the judge before it can be filed. You will probably be the one doing the courthouse run daily this summer, so it will be a good opportunity to get acquainted."

"There's so much to learn. Thanks for your help." Erin smiled at the woman she knew would be a wealth of information.

"Anytime. Toni is very proud of you and says you will make a great attorney. She should know. Besides, us girls need to stick together sometimes." Janice ran back toward the brick building.

Walking past the receptionist's desk, Stephanie again avoided Erin's eyes. Erin wondered if the woman ever smiled.

"See Sara and finish your paperwork before you go home this evening." Stephanie turned back and nodded toward Erin and then pushed the button on her ear piece answering the phone.

Erin spent the rest of the day working on the endless mound of papers allowing her to be employed as the light began to dim outside the building.

"You still working on that?" Toni stood in the door with her high heels in hand. "I don't know about you, but I'm about beat."

"I'm almost finished but need to watch some videos on harassment or something."

Toni put her hand to her mouth covering a yawn, sighed and shook her head turning to go. "I'm calling your mom and ordering some Chinese take-out. Things will go faster if you have a friend to help you watch those award-winning movies."

Chapter 7

Erin walked through the back door of the house where she lived with her mother. The TV on, Mom had a casserole in the oven.

"Hi, honey!" Mom called from the living room. "How was the first day at work?"

"I'm exhausted, but a good day," Erin said on the way to the bedroom to change.

"Bernadette called. She wants you to call her back." Alice flipped the channels on the television.

"She called my cell too. I'll change and call her. Casserole smells good."

"There's still some in the oven if you want it. It's a new recipe from Felicity."

"Thanks, but I ate with Aunt Toni." Erin held the phone to her ear as she pulled off the blouse she felt she had worn too long. Office work could be as dirty as flower shops.

"Wanna' drive by the lake and see what's going on?" Bernadette's voice on the other end of the line spoke with more energy than Erin felt.

"Is there a party? Cause I really don't want to deal with a bunch of drunk teenagers tonight," Erin replied.

"You sound like an old lady!" Bernadette giggled.

"I just don't want to deal with it. I've had enough for one day."

"No, the guys just wanted to get out. We can take

my car," Bernadette said. "And if we find a party, we'll just keep driving. What do you say, us and the guys, little moonlit walk on the beach?"

"I'll get my trunks." Erin could hear Rob's voice on the other end.

"I'm not swimming. I don't trust that lake after dark. Last time I found a snake and he almost got me." Steve chimed in.

"It was a stick." Bernadette spoke to the people who were with her.

"Oh yeah? It had fangs," Steve replied in the background.

"You could see the fangs in the dark, but not the snake," Rob hassled. Erin knew Rob and Steve were with Bernadette making their conversation impossible.

"I'm not going back in that water after dark." Steve again.

"I don't want to swim either, just hang out at the lake. I may not get too many chances for a while since I'm working all the time." Erin pulled the tank top over her head while she talked to her friend. Her work clothes lay on the bed.

"Sorry for the background noise. You know they're crazy."

"Yes, I'm changing clothes now. See you soon." Erin clicked off the phone and walked to the front of the house.

"Mom," Erin called as she headed to the kitchen. "We're going for a drive up by the lake in Bernadette's car."

"I thought you were tired?" Mom changed channels.

"I am but I don't get to see my friends that much

anymore." Erin walked into the living room where her mother sat watching television. It occurred to her how the friends she saw daily in school now she only saw occasionally.

"Okay, but don't be late. You have to go to work in the morning."

"I won't." Erin kissed her mother's cheek as she heard Bernadette's horn honk. In the small town where they lived, Bernadette lived right around the corner.

School out, the cove they normally visited jumped with kids enjoying the summer nights. Music blared, and laughter echoed across the still waters. Erin felt too tired to dance and most of those kids were not her friends. The people she considered friends were in the car with her.

Thankfully, Bernadette kept driving. The lake, large, held a secret place the girls went to when they were young. It had a great view of the mansions on the other side. The part of the lake where they were not welcome. Todd and his family owned one of them. Erin didn't know which one.

Walking down to the water, Rob immediately picked up stones and tossed them in, expertly skipping a few by moonlight.

"What is there about water that is so attractive? I mean why am I so drawn to it?" Erin climbed up a boulder bigger than her car, if she could see the part under the soil, and sat on the top viewing the water after dark. She could hear Bernadette teasing Rob about snakes back at the car. Her best friends and a moonlit night by the lake—could things get any better? Rob sat down beside her with his handful of rocks. The moon shone across water like glass. Not a ripple on the lake except where Rob tossed the pebbles. Even the water seemed to be resting from the day.

"I think mankind has always been drawn to water. We need it to live. And if scientists are right, we may have evolved from it."

"I used to be a tadpole." Erin smiled in the dark at her friend.

"Something like that. So, you'll be driving into Tulsa every day for work?" He changed the subject quickly.

"I guess. Until school starts, then part time."

"Can I buy you lunch sometime? You know, come by the office and take you to lunch?"

Squealing came from the car and peals of laughter. Bernadette continued to drive poor Steve crazy with snake stories.

"Should we invite the nutcases?" She nodded toward the noise.

"How about just us? I mean they're great and all, but we never have any time alone." He reached up and touched her face, running his finger down her jawline and across her lips. She shivered. He slowly leaned in brushing his lips across the area traced by his finger. Then again, kissing her more urgently this time. Surprisingly she found she liked it. Her friend that she worked with at the grocery store and went to school with, kissed her in the moonlight—like a boyfriend. It took a minute before Erin realized. Rob kissed her! Did she want that?

"Rob." she backed up as he leaned in again. "I really don't think this is a good idea."

"I think it is a great idea." Rob leaned toward her smiling.

"No, stop." She stood quickly, pulling away from him.

"I'm sorry, I didn't mean to upset you." He stood up on the boulder.

"I'm not upset. It's just that I don't want a relationship. I thought you understood that. I'm going to school in the fall and I can't get distracted and end up like my mother."

"Erin, I'm not trying to stop you from doing the things in life you want to do. And I'm sure not asking you to marry me. I just kissed you." Rob tossed the pebbles out into the water.

"I know how this works. I get involved with some guy and all my hopes and dreams go out the window." Erin could remember her mother talking about getting married and pregnant too early many times. Her mom said she should get an education, and Erin knew she was right.

"Like I said, I only kissed you, I will admit it's something I have wanted to do for a long time, but I didn't want a fight. I just like being around you."

"I like being around you too, but the last thing I want is to end up like my mom—married and a mother by nineteen. I am going to law school."

"And I am going to be an engineer. I'm going to school on a work study program—not like some people who have a full ride. I'll have to work my way through."

"I'm working too."

"Yea, at a law office." He laughed. "I'll probably be at a sandwich shop. Really, I'm happy for you. And if you want to be just friends, I can live with that. I won't bother you anymore. I don't want to get between you and your dreams." He stood with a dejected expression on his face.

"It's not you. It is just the situation. I guess I'm a little bit scared about not reaching my goals. But for now, at least, will you just be my friend?"

"Snake! Snake!" Bernadette yelled laughing.

"Just stop it!" Steve yelled back.

"Yeah, and I'll be a better friend than those two." Rob grabbed her hand and helped her down from the rock. They walked back to the car hand in hand.

Chapter 8

N. Robert Cronkite—Bobby to his friends—had been a lawyer for almost forty years. He'd seen it all. People didn't surprise him anymore. Always a defense attorney, he sometimes wondered why. Well, he knew why. Money. The client had the right to counsel and the attorneys they paid for were better than the ones the court appointed. At least more experienced. Often the court-appointed ones were just trying to make a buck until they could gather a clientele and not have to live off the bread and water handed down by some judge.

But, this case disgusted him more than any before or since. The mother in this case was the dredge of humanity. Normally in domestic cases, the father ran, and the mother sued. But not this time. This time, the mother ran. And she took the child. Dad wanted more than his day in court. He would pay attorney fees, child support, court costs—he even offered to pay the mother to go away—even though they wouldn't tell the court. Mortgaged to the hilt, still he wouldn't quit.

He had to find his son. Would Cronkite have felt any different? The mother took the child out of the state and changed his name just to keep him away from the father, and who knew what else she'd done to the boy. Brainwashing they used to call it. Washing all the good stuff out and replacing it with the mother's own brand of craziness. She suffered from paranoia—Bobby pressed the court to have her tested last time they found her.

They bugged her shabby hotel room—even though that evidence wouldn't hold up in court—and later he sat down with the client to review the tape. He could barely understand the garbled words.

*"Now remember, your name is Eric this time. Eric Smith and you are from California."* You could hear the sound of a zipper. *"You might need a jacket today, it's a little cool."*

*"Momma, I'm tired of changing my name. And I want to go home."*

*"You are home, honey. We live here in Oregon now. I work at the diner just down the street and you go to school right around the corner. We'll be fine."*

*"But what about Dad? How will he find us?"* The childlike voice sounded strained.

*"I told you, your dad always knows where we are, and he'll come visit soon."*

The utterly calm-sounding woman made Cronkite's blood run cold. How could she be so calculating? There were plenty of fathers who ran out, but not this one. In this case, the mother just wanted to get back at the boy's father for the divorce. She would continue to run just to see to it that the father had no access to his biological son. One she said he never wanted in the first place. She was wrong.

Cronkite called this his pet case, but actually it was a nightmare—one that played over and over in his mind and kept him up at night. He'd tracked the mother with the help of a young paralegal who no longer worked for the firm. She secured affidavits from some of the people the mother knew who finally turned against her.

Even her relatives began to help the father out—if it didn't inconvenience them too much. Now, he'd lost her again. Time to get back to work on the case, and Cronkite and the father knew it had to happen soon.

A new girl just joined the firm. Erin, a student who showed promise. Maybe he would take advantage of her youth and energy and put her to work to see if she could find the mother. Kids and computers. They could do anything.

Chapter 9

Sally stared at her reflection in the mirror. Her hair and makeup perfect, she slipped into blue stiletto heels matching her dress. Todd liked her to dress up. She adjusted the thong panties feeling the result of the Brazilian bikini wax—another thing Todd insisted on. She had no idea where they were going tonight but knew how the evening would end up. They would have sex—probably somewhere outdoors or in his car. Todd would insist upon it. She liked having sex with him, but if you dated Todd Newman, he expected it. Everyone knew that. Well, at least all the girls he had dated knew that, even though some didn't talk about it. But she knew how to please him. She planned to marry this one, then she and Mom would be set for life. He didn't know that yet, but she would find a way.

She knew the roar of his vintage 1974 midnight blue Alpha Romeo Spider Veloce with the black rag top even before it pulled to the curb outside her house. The car might be the only thing he truly loved. She ran for the door. "See you later, Mom." She smiled on her way out the door. He sat staring forward revving the engine of the sports car.

"How are you, sweetie?" She kissed him on the cheek, sliding into the leather seats. Her head snapped back as he quickly pulled away from the curb and sped downtown without a word.

\*\*\*\*

By Saturday morning Rob hadn't seen Erin in almost a week. The new job kept her busy, but he told her he would fix her car door hinges. If he could get them done before his shift this afternoon, it would be better for him. He was scheduled to work afternoons this weekend. The grocery store would be busy due to the Independence Day holiday. Everyone needed hot dogs and hamburgers for family barbeques—and then there were the summer lake people. The little town by the lake always doubled in size during warm weather and everyone had to eat.

Pulling into the driveway of the white bungalow Erin shared with her mother, he saw her car in the driveway. She never locked it at home even though he wished she would. He hoped she at least locked it when she left it in the law office parking lot in Tulsa. Having grown up in a small town, Erin did not have to worry so much about her neighbors as in the big city.

Popping the trunk of his own car, he pulled out a few tools and opened Erin's screeching car doors. The creak could wake the dead. The can of WD 40 in hand he sprayed the hinges of the driver's side door letting it set for a moment when the screen door slammed, and Erin walked out barefoot in cut-offs. Hair in a ponytail, she carried two coffee cups. She smiled as she walked his way.

"My knight in shining armor. Again."

Rob could not help but smile back at that face.

"Good morning. I hoped I didn't wake you with the squeaking car door."

"Mom and I were up. She left for the shop a while ago. Are you working today?"

"This afternoon." He swung the door back and forth a few times and then sprayed it again with grease this time. "I get off at nine. Want to go get something to eat after work? Or just drive by the lake or something? I never see you anymore." He sipped the coffee she handed him.

"Sure. Maybe we can take some sandwiches down to the lake or something. Have you got work study figured out yet?"

Rob walked around to the other side of the car and began the process all over again. "I'll be working in the library first semester. I don't know after that. It will be a good fit though. I'll spend most of my time there or in the engineering lab anyway."

"Good." Erin touched her tongue to the hot liquid.

"What about you? Will you still work part time for the law office? I hope they give you time to study."

"They have to. Besides, I am learning so much, it will help make law school a breeze."

"Well, it is a long time until law school. You have to get the bachelor's first." He put the tools away he never used and wiped his hands on the rag hanging from his jean pocket. Car doors needed a little TLC now and then. "In the meantime, how about I pick you up after I get off?"

"Sure, I'll fix something to eat and we can go down to the cove. I really don't know how to thank you for all the things you do for me and the car."

"Well, maybe we can think of something." Rob smiled around the coffee cup as he sipped.

"What time do you have to be at work? Do you have time to sit on the porch swing for a while and talk?" Erin nodded at the porch.

"Sure. I don't go in until one."

"Do you have your classes set up?" Erin walked to the swing her father hung on the front porch years ago. She couldn't remember it not being there. She often sat between her parents after dinner in the evenings swinging back and forth as they discussed their days. Those were good times and the swing always felt like home.

"Yeah, I got online and enrolled last week. I got most of the ones I wanted. How about you?"

"Yeah, I'm enrolled. I managed to CLEP out of some of the basics. Bernadette and I are planning to study together a lot this semester since we're taking some of the same courses. Maybe you would like to join us?"

"Sure. Are you studying on campus? I mean of the four of us, you are the only one not living there."

"Probably the library or something. Or we could do it in Bernadette's room if her roommate is gone."

"Sure, let's plan on it." Rob drained the coffee cup. "I need to get some things done before work. Pick you up a little after nine tonight?"

"I'll be ready, and I'll make us something to eat." She walked down the steps to his car with him and waved goodbye as he backed out of the driveway. Such a good guy and he obviously liked her.

The phone in her pocket rang as she headed back in the house with the empty coffee cups. The screen just read "Toni."

"Hi, Aunt Toni!"

"Hey, sweetie." Toni's voice still retained the Oklahoma drawl when she talked to her family. The courtroom voice, a distant memory. "Are you busy?

Want to come over and help me clean out my closet?"

"Clean out your closet?" Erin walked in the house with the cups.

"Yeah, you know stuff to wear to work. I've got to get rid of some things and I thought you might want something else besides that cute little navy skirt to wear."

"I have been wearing it a lot."

"Not that anyone would notice, but if you're not busy, maybe we could work on the closet together and get some take-out or something. Unless you have other plans. Besides, I haven't gotten you a birthday present yet."

"Good grief. I haven't even thought about my birthday this year. I've been so busy. Well, I need to be back home before nine. I sort of have a date."

"Oh my! A date? Anyone I know?" Toni's voice on the other end took on a southern bell drawl.

"Yeah, just Rob. We're going down by the lake and I promised to bring something to eat He's been so good to me lately working on my car and stuff."

"He's a nice guy. You be careful. You know how nice guys can be."

Erin could hear the smile in her aunt's voice and she giggled. "You mean the ones that call your dad sir and then try to chew the rivets off your jeans?" An old joke at her house—something her mom and aunt used to quote from an equally ancient movie.

"Well, nineteen isn't the landmark we put on eighteen, but you still have a birthday before school starts and you need some new work clothes. Besides, I need to get rid of some stuff. It will be a win-win for both of us."

"Okay, let me finish cleaning up the kitchen. Mom's working so I'm cleaning house. I'll be over in about an hour." Erin clicked off the phone and began to unload the dishwasher.

Erin pulled into the parking garage of the luxury apartments in downtown Tulsa only a few blocks from the courthouse and law firm. Her aunt's career her life, she lived it—and she lived close to it.

Taking the elevator up, she walked down the hall and rang the bell. Aunt Toni, barefoot in jeans and a t-shirt, answered quickly. "Come in sweetie and try not to trip over anything."

The beautiful apartment overlooking downtown Tulsa resembled the aftermath of a tornado. There were clothes strewn over every chair and ottoman creating a path to the bedroom.

"Okay, the good stuff is still in the bedroom for you to check out. A lot of this is going to the homeless shelter in town and there are still things hanging up in the closet. I wanted you to have the first choice though. Some of it is too old for you, but you might be able to make it work with some different accessories. I have no idea why I have so many black pants and skirts. But, they go with everything. And there are some evening dresses you might want to see too. There will be parties coming up that the firm throws at the country club and you'll be invited." Toni gestured toward the closet.

The scene overwhelming, Toni piled all the skirts together and pants in another pile. Sweaters were on the love seat in the corner of the room and shoes were everywhere. The top of the dresser also held jewelry and scarves. And hanging in the middle of the closet— the silver dress that Bernadette's mother beautifully mended. Only Erin knew its history.

"You'll need a suit or two when you go to court for hearings. I understand Bobby wants you to help him out with an upcoming trial. Has he mentioned that to you? He needs to because you will have to get acquainted with the discovery documents if you are going to be of any help."

"I'm going to court? You mean for something other than filing documents at the courthouse?"

"Bobby said he wanted you, and what Bobby wants, Bobby gets. His name is on the door."

"Really? That's cool. What kind of case is it?" Erin knew she wanted in on the case whatever the kind.

"You'll have to talk to him about that. Now over here are the evening dresses. You can have that silver one you like."

"No thanks. But the slinky green one is pretty." Erin fingered the lighter than air deep green chiffon with sequins. She never even dreamed of owning something so exquisite.

"You going to tell me what happened that night? You didn't fall down. I could tell by your face that night. It was that Newman kid wasn't it? He tear your dress?"

"He's a jerk." Erin glanced up from the dress at her aunt.

"Yeah, so's his old man. But he's a client with money so we try to keep him happy. Not that I wouldn't love to beat him up in a courtroom if he hurt you in any way." Toni stood with her arms crossed over her chest staring down her niece like a witness on a stand.

"I don't know about his dad, but Todd is a bully. He likes to show off for his friends. He doesn't really like anyone but himself and the rumors are that he really doesn't like girls. I don't mean he likes guys—you know—just that he is rough on his girlfriends. I started hearing things about him after the prom." Erin had not talked about the night of the prom for months.

"Did he hurt you that night?"

"Not really, just embarrassed me."

"Well, if he ever hurts or embarrasses you again, I want to know about it. I've got plenty of dirt on his dad and I'm not above using it. Now, these shoes over here might be something you could use for everyday wear."

They spent the afternoon going through the enormous piles of clothes—none from the local discount chains—and Erin started a pile of her own to take home, avoiding the silver dress. Heaps of clothes around boxes of Chinese takeout filled the apartment and Erin relaxed with her aunt enjoying the moment. The women adored each other. Shadows in the apartment grew longer as summer evenings began much later than the rest of the year when Erin realized the time.

"Oh, it's late! I've got to go. I haven't fixed anything for the picnic and I don't want to be late. Rob has been so kind to me lately working on my car and everything." Erin grabbed stacks of clothes as she talked.

"Just grab something on the way home. There are sandwich shops between here and your house. Don't panic, I'll help you. Let me find some shoes."

"Well, there are shoes everywhere, shouldn't be a problem."

Erin and Toni boxed up shoes and purses and grabbed clothes on hangers. They filled the elevator and then ran for the car in the garage making several trips. Soon the trunk and back seat were overfull. The tiny car barely had room for Erin in the front and the sandwiches purchased along the way.

Screeching to a halt in the driveway, Erin saw Rob's car at the curb. He sat on the swing with her mother holding a glass of iced tea. They were talking and laughing like old friends.

"You're late," Alice pointed out as Erin walked up to the porch with the food. "And this boy is starving. I tried to feed him, but he wanted to wait for you."

"I'm sorry. Aunt Toni and I got carried away. The whole car is full of clothes. I don't know where I'm going to put them all." Erin pointed to the car to prove her story.

"That's okay. Your mom was just telling me stories about you as a little girl. You used to get so greasy in your dad's garage she couldn't get you clean for weeks. With all that time in the garage, how come you don't take better care of your car?" Rob smiled as he shared the joke with Alice.

"Probably because I'm so busy. I have sandwiches. Still want to go down by the lake?"

"Sure." Rob stood from the swing and Alice followed. She took the glass from his hands. "You kids have a good time and be careful around the water."

"Bye, Mom." Erin lightly pecked her mother on the cheek and ran for Rob's car with the sack, handing the drinks to him along the way. The overfilled car waited in the driveway, until the next day to be emptied.

\*\*\*\*

Erin sat on the blanket in the moonlight munching a submarine sandwich and chips. The tree frogs serenaded all who would listen, and the occasional mosquito buzzed past her ear. Rob finished his sandwich and leaned back on his elbows raising his head to see the stars and sighed.

"I can't believe how much I'm going to miss this place. I spent most of my life waiting to get out of this little one-horse town and now I'm thinking how much I'll miss it."

"You'll miss the town or the lake?" Erin drained the last of the soda with a slurp.

"The lake I think. The town is—well the town. It's the lake I really love. I think I want to build a house on a lake someday after I'm finished with school and settled in."

"You mean you want a lake house when you grow up?" He could see her smile even in the dark. He knew she loved to poke at him to see how he would react.

"Yeah, when I grow up. Like when I grow up, become an engineer, and pay off my giant student loans, I'd like to live on a lake or something. You know, with the wife and kids."

"The wife and kids, huh? You gettin' married Anderson?"

"Maybe."

"Anyone in mind?"

"Maybe." He reached over and lifted her chin. Even in the dark he could still see the sparkle in her eyes and knew she kidded him. "I might have someone in mind. How about you?" He leaned in close to kiss her.

Just before he reached her lips, she spoke.

"You ask me a question and then try to shut me up? You know I don't shut up easily."

"Well, I guess I'll have to try harder." This time he made contact. Lightly he brushed her lips with his and then kissed them lightly. She didn't pull away. He kissed her again, this time more passionately pulling her close. She exhaled melting into him and he slowly pushed her back onto the blanket—when frigid liquid hit his stomach and rolled down his pants. The soda he barely touched spilled out and across the blanket as they crushed the flimsy wax-coated cup with the weight of their bodies.

"Oh cold!" Erin jumped up brushing the ice off her t-shirt giggling. "What did you do Anderson? Where did that ice come from?"

"I think that was my drink. I didn't know where it went in the dark. I forgot where I put it. Sorry. Way to kill a mood!"

Rob jerked his head behind him when the heavy breathing started in the rustling bushes. He grabbed Erin's hand and dragged her toward the car just as the body burst forth from the brush. A girl in a torn blue dress tripped on the blanket and fell face-first into the icy mess letting out a puff of air as she hit the ground. She quickly got to her feet and climbed up the hill into the two of them in a panic, shoving them apart as if she didn't realize they were there. Then kept climbing.

"Sally?" Erin instantly grabbed Rob's hand again. "Sally? Sally Elkman! Sally are you okay?" Erin ran after the girl, pulling Rob behind her.

The girl stopped in her tracks. Slowly she turned and stared out at the lake and then lowered her gaze to Erin and Rob.

"Are you okay?" Erin asked again. "It's Erin Sampson from school."

The girl's face suddenly changed, as recognition appeared.

"Erin. What are you doing out here?" Sally tried to smooth her dress.

"We were having a picnic. What happened to you? Are you okay?" Erin didn't like Sally, but she would help her if she needed it.

The beam of light from the road temporarily blinded them and Rob put his hand up to shade his eyes. The roar of the engine revved once, then twice. Rob recognized the engine of the Alpha. Only one person around Mannford drove an Alpha Romeo.

Sally turned without a word and climbed the rest of the way to the top of the hill, clamored in the door of the vehicle, and the sports car screeched down the road, laying rubber as it went.

## Chapter 10

Sara stood with her arms folded over her chest, waiting when Erin arrived at work on Monday. The peaceful walk from the parking lot in the unusually cool summer morning filled with the song birds and a blue sky had her in a good mood. But her morning was about to heat up. Stephanie, already on the phone with her legs crossed, had a nail file in her hand. She turned her back on Erin when she walked in.

"Don't get too comfortable." Sara grabbed Erin's arm and pulled her down the hall. "I'm putting you in this conference room." She opened the door, gesturing. "Bobby asked me to pull these files for you to review. He'll be in later to tell you what it is he needs you to find. I think Nathan will be out today, but if he appears—don't let him run you off this time. Send him packin'. Bobby has scheduled this room for the week." Sara walked out the door leaving Erin staring at the files.

A laptop sat at the end of the boardroom table plugged in and a tower of files stood sentinel beside a legal pad. Erin stared at the unbelievably tall stack of folders wondering what to do with them. The tabs were marked "Dauber v Little FD 2010-598." Piled on the table were at least fifteen of them and they were all marked 1 of 15, 2 of 15, etc. How could all these files belong to one case? Then she saw the three bank boxes on the floor and knew the stack did not end on the table. The box lid had the same file name, and in bold letters "DISCOVERY" written on top. She flipped off the lids and found there were infinitely more files. What had she gotten herself into?

"Well, little girl, what do you think?" Without a noise N. Robert Cronkite stood before her in a navy jacket and gray pants. His red tie rolled down over his ample belly and white shirt. His hair matched the shirt as it lay over his collar in need of a trim and the piercing blue eyes danced when he spoke. Erin wondered if he made fun of her age.

"I think there are a lot of files here with the same name on them." Erin raised her head from the pile to the man in the doorway.

"Very astute. And you didn't run and hide. I like that." Cronkite looked Erin over.

"Why would I hide?" Erin asked the man who once thought she delivered office supplies and told her to go around to the back. Like her aunt said, his name was on the door. A lawyer before her birth, maybe longer than her mother had been alive. He had seen it all, and there he stood in front of her wanting her help.

"This case has been going on for some time. The year shows you when it was filed, and the FD means it is a family divorce. But that's not important. What is important is the child custody that went along with the divorce. How good are you with a computer? Most young people can find anything on a computer. We have an account with People Search—ask Sara for the info—and I need you to find this mother, again. You need to know she is crazy as a loon and her ex is a desperate man. He wants his child back and is afraid for the child's safety. He has a right to be scared. I don't think she has hurt the child physically. But mentally, he is probably already scarred for life. He's grade school age already. So, she's had many years to warp his sense of the world. It will take you a while, but scan through these files in numerical order and get a feel for what has been happening and where she has taken the child. See if you can find a trend as to where she has been and maybe where she'll go next, that's what we want to find. Then run a search on her. We need to know where she is now. Write it on the legal pad, make a spreadsheet on the computer, I don't care how you keep track, but make a chart that you can explain to me later. And let me know if you have questions." Cronkite nodded his head and turned walking out the door leaving her with the mountain of paperwork in front of her.

She opened the first file and found an index on one side and emails on the other.

"The index lists all the pleadings that have been filed in the case." Sara stood in the doorway and handed Erin a bottle of water. "They're in order with the latest on top. If you start reading from the bottom, you can see how the case has progressed."

"There's a novel here!"

"More than a novel. You have a lot to read and a lot to find. But, Bobby has faith in you, so I know you can do it. You might also learn a lot from the emails and documents on the other side of the file. They should be in chronological order too. Depositions were taken. Their transcripts are in the box. You will find them in the discovery boxes along with other evidence. They're in a specific order so don't mess it up. I put some yellow stickies on the important pleadings. Read them first and you will get a feel for what has gone on here. This case has kept Bobby up at night. It's one he just can't let go. It seems the mother ran off again, and so far, the father hasn't found her. That is where we come in. Here's our account info for People Search and as usual, if you need anything don't hesitate to ask." Sara handed a scrap of paper across the table with passwords and logins to Erin and then went back to her desk.

Opening the bottle of water, Erin read the first document marked with a yellow sticky note. Legal documents were alien to her; but the first one filed in the case according to the date told her a lot about the case and why they filed it.

She read into the morning making notes on the legal pad. The divorce granted, the parents had joint custody over the child who lived primarily with the mother. The father was given visitation rights. Then the trouble began. The mother quickly left town and remained unavailable for many months, running with his child.

Opening the laptop, Erin started a spreadsheet entering the date they found the mother and where. She saved the new file on the computer to its desktop. It could be moved later when she understood more about what she needed to do. Just as she clicked save, the door to the boardroom swung open with a bang.

"Well hi there! We meet again. Erin, isn't it?"

Nathan stood filling the door frame. He was an attractive man in his forties with chestnut brown hair and dark eyes. His face showed one dimple when he smiled his crooked smile. Erin didn't trust that smile.

His athletic build said he spent some time in the gym, not just at a computer.

"Yes, I'm Erin. Mr. Cronkite and Sara put me in here to work on this case."

Nathan walked to the table and picked up the file she had open, reading the label on the side, then leaned over her shoulder studying the computer screen. "Oh yeah, ol' Bobby loves this one. Well, honey, you're gonna have to move again. I have a meeting."

"Sara said that Mr. Cronkite has this room booked all week."

"Sara said, huh? Well, Sara doesn't own this place and just because you're Toni's niece doesn't give you any special privileges. Go get a cart and move this stuff out, my client will be here any moment."

Erin felt her face flush and she tried not to allow him to see her hands shaking. "Sara said not to let you run me out again." She knew her voice shook. "She also said there were other conference rooms available if you need one." Erin hoped her nervousness did not show as she stood staring Nathan in the eye. But she knew it did.

"Trouble Nathan?" An overweight man stood in the hallway looking in. He seemed oddly familiar, but Erin had no idea where she might have seen him before. His bulbous nose crisscrossed with the telltale spider veins of a long time alcoholic, and the blue Polo shirt he wore told of his affluence—it had an emblem of the local country club embroidered on the chest pocket. Then it hit her. He was an older and fatter version of Todd Newman.

"No Howard, no problem. Janice, get Howard some coffee and set him in my office, I'll be right there." Nathan's assistant appeared as if from nowhere and led the client down the hall just as Cronkite walked in from the other direction.

"Nate, how goes it this morning? I have Erin in here working on my pet project. I'm sure you can take Newman into another conference room. We have this one tied up right now." Robert Cronkite appeared in the doorway, smiled, and patted Nathan on the shoulder in a fatherly fashion. Erin wondered if they were friends, but everyone knew Cronkite ran the office with an iron fist.

Cronkite's office sat across on the other side of the building, but Sara told her he always had his finger on the pulse of the firm. He knew everything that went on. It made Erin nervous at first. However, he had sided with her—at least for the moment.

Nathan nodded and left without a word, glancing back at Erin one last time.

The room was deathly quiet.

"Um, Mr. Cronkite, I found some things I wanted to show you if you have time." Erin opened the file on the desktop of the computer. He leaned in close to see her work.

"The mother initially left Oklahoma for Kansas— barely across the state line from the boy's father, but far enough away that he could not find them. From Kansas, she went to Missouri and then later to Nevada. I'm unclear how many other places she might have lived as she and the child were on the run, but the father, hot on her trail found people who knew where she went. Then he hit a brick wall when the mother's friends quit talking to him." Erin raised her head considering the man she idolized and found him smiling at her.

"Good job. I knew you could do it. Keep up the good work." He turned and disappeared again.

Erin smiled with satisfaction. Maybe she'd fit in here yet. With Nathan and Cronkite gone, she went back to her notes—and the music started next door. The theme from the Broadway musical *Cats* could only mean one thing. Ann arrived. Ann, a semi-retired worker, only came in three partial days a week, but like her days, her selection of music short. She still had a CD player in her office from the old days and Erin knew once it started playing it would be non-stop, all day long. For some reason she really loved that music, or she only owned one CD. Ann, always kind to Erin, still played her music. Sara told her that Ann had a daughter who performed on Broadway and Erin wondered if she was a cast member of *Cats*. Some days the music became so monotonous to not even be heard anymore. Not today.

Reaching into her purse, Erin pulled out her iPod and plugged into her own music. Again, interrupted by a presence in the doorway, she pulled one earbud out and left it dangling.

Jimmy filled the doorway in a very different way than Mr. Newman. Jimmy, a body builder who worked exclusively on title work, could be found at the gym when not in the office. His physique like a Mr. Universe contestant in his T-shirt and shorts, Erin wondered what he wore in the winter.

"Morning. Bobby got you busy? I didn't know this conference room was occupied. I'll go down the hall."

Erin smiled at the man in the doorway. A lawyer without a suit. But he never went to court, so he just came to work comfortably. "Mr. Cronkite has me working on some files."

"Well, don't let me bother you." He walked off down the hall, his massive arms bulged out from the shoulders unable to touch his body as he walked away. A gentle giant type, he was not what Erin always thought of as a lawyer. She realized they were just people with different personalities who all chose the same profession. Sara said if anyone ever needed title work done they should turn to Jimmy and his non-traditional work style. Erin believed her.

The People Search found nothing as Erin poured over documents trying to find Karen Little. She found her social security number in the cover sheet for the original petition filed in the divorce—but was the address current? She charted out in Excel all the places the woman moved in the last few years. Why was she running and trying so hard to keep the father from seeing his child? And why in the direction she chose? Did she have family in the areas she moved to? Various search engines all hit the same snag. No current address and no indication if she continued to move on.

Erin worked into the morning when the phone rang.

"This is Erin," she said in to the phone not knowing how to answer it.

"Your boyfriend is here," Stephanie said teasing her.

"Boyfriend?"

"Rob. He says his name is Rob and you two have a lunch date?"

Oh crap! She had forgotten Rob and her promise to go to lunch with him today. "Tell him I'll be right there." Erin hung up the phone and closed the laptop saving her work, certain the documents and computer would be safe in the conference room. She grabbed her purse and left.

Once outside, Erin relaxed. "I'm sorry. I got kinda caught up in a case and didn't realize the time. Where are we going?"

"Anywhere you want." Rob smiled. "Big case?"

"Well, could be." Knowing she couldn't talk about cases she worked on, she steered him away from the subject.

"There's a sandwich shop within walking distance and we won't have to move the car." She grabbed his arm and guided him across the street.

Seated in the busy lunch crowd, Erin munched the tuna sandwich and chips. Rob stared at her across the table.

"Nice place you work. But the woman up front is a little stiff."

"Stephanie? Yeah, stiff is one way to put it. She doesn't like me; I don't know why really. I haven't done anything to make her mad, but she's been that way since I got here."

"You're the niece of a partner and got the job through your aunt." Rob slurped his drink.

"That's not my fault."

"No, just sayin' some people are like that. They think you didn't work to get where you are."

"Oh, I'm working all right." Erin laughed and poked the last of the sandwich in her mouth. "I didn't even realize how hungry I'd gotten."

"You forgot our date, didn't you?" He glanced at her out of the corner of his eyes.

"No, I didn't forget, it's just…"

"You forgot. So, I guess we'll just have to do it again then. You obviously work too hard and need a break." He wiped his mouth with the paper napkin.

"Okay, I forgot, I'm sorry. And yes, I'm working hard, but I do love it." Erin smiled at the boy who chased her, and she constantly put off. She had no idea why he continued to come around.

"Okay, you're forgiven, but just this once. Like I said, we'll have to do it again now." He smiled slightly and picked up her trash carrying it to the garbage near the door. "You ready? I know you have work to do."

"What about you? Are you working today?" Erin slid her hand through the crook in his arm as they walked out the door.

"Off today. Think I'll change the oil in my car. You know, changing oil—stuff you are supposed to do to a vehicle now and then?"

"I've heard of that. A good friend of mine did it for me recently."

## Chapter 11

Brent Taylor had done nothing but work in a grocery store all his life. His father, always a produce manager, convinced his son it was the thing to do. He began his career in high school bagging groceries. Not a bad job, just a job—and his supervisors thought he did it well. Recently he'd moved up from an assistant manager to the manager of the new store in Mannford. The employees liked him—well at least most of them did—if they did their jobs. And the bonuses kept coming in from corporate. His ex-wife let him see the kids often. They were good kids—kids from another divorced home—but what kids weren't, these days?

When they offered him the new Mannford store, he saw it as a great opportunity—and he grabbed it. Assistant Manager could only go so far, but once he had his own store to manage, it was a short step to Regional Manager. He could still see his kids in Tulsa on the weekends when they didn't have activities that kept them busy. And college for them was right around the corner—an expense Brent could only imagine. Only two years apart, there would be at least six years of tuition and expenses if they made it through in four years each and didn't want to pursue a graduate degree. He had to go. So, he packed up his few possessions and left the apartment in the big city for a duplex in a small town.

The day the petite blonde came in for an interview to manage the flower shop he stood up and took notice. The first woman he had been attracted to since his divorce from Susan. Never again, he told himself. He'd be a dad, a grocer, and that would be enough. One agonizing heart-break per lifetime, thank you very much. But still, he asked around and found her widowed with a teenaged daughter. She once owned a flower shop that probably went under because of the new one in town. Not very friendly—all business. But who could blame her? She lost her livelihood due to a major corporation undercutting her prices. She needed the job but didn't have to be best friends with her boss. He wouldn't press her. But he did bring her doughnuts on occasion when she came to the Monday morning meetings. Of course, they came from the bakery in the store, and he brought enough for all the department managers, but really, they were for her. He hoped that she would warm up eventually and maybe someday he would see that welcoming smile that she displayed to the customers aimed at him.

His dad had been a pretty good shade-tree mechanic and taught Brent all he knew. He could change his own oil, trade out a battery, or do a brake job now and then—stuff not too difficult. So, when he found Alice standing by her car in the parking lot with the hood up staring intently into its cavernous mouth, he thought it might be his lucky day. She needed help.

"Not running?" He walked up beside her as she stared vacantly under the hood.

"It won't even turn over. It worked fine this morning. I have no idea what's wrong."

He leaned over and wiggled the wires that

connected the battery to the engine. Not much corrosion on the contacts.

"Can I try something?" he asked before loosening the connection to the battery.

"Of course, anything. I don't know what to do."

He reached over and unhooked the battery connections and then attached them once more. "There, see if that did any good. Try to start it."

Alice climbed in the car and turned the key. Nothing. Not even a grunt.

"Could be the battery. How old is it?"

Alice opened the door to the glove box and dug through a mound of paperwork until she found the receipt for the battery. She scanned down the page.

"It is a two-year battery and it's been about two years. Why does this happen to me when Erin is out of town? I guess I'll have to have it towed."

"Well, I could take the battery out and we could take it over to the auto parts store and have them put it on a tester. No need for a tow charge if you don't have to."

"No really, that's not necessary. I'll call my friend Felicity and she can come get me."

"Well, that won't help you get the car started. Let me take it to get it checked."

"No really, it is not necessary. Felicity can come get me…" She thumbed through her cell phone scanning her contacts.

"Okay, but it's no trouble." Brent wiped his hands on the seat of his jeans.

"Felicity, call me back when you get this. I'm stranded at work and the car won't start." She clicked off the phone and regarded at her boss. "Well, maybe if it isn't too much trouble. I guess my friend is busy."

"No trouble at all. Glad to help."

With the battery in the back of his pickup, Brent held the door open for Alice and she climbed in wearing the pants and shirt she wore to work. Once inside the pickup she took off the apron that covered her blouse and folded it in the seat between them.

"I normally leave that at work, but I planned to wash it this evening. By the way, thanks so much for helping me out. I hate being stranded. It is such a vulnerable feeling. My husband always took care of things like this and I just hate feeling inept."

"You're not inept. My ex-wife couldn't even find the gas cap when we were married. I'm sure she could not open a hood or find a battery."

"Well, I opened the hood, but had no idea what to look for." She picked at her shirt tail nervously.

"So, you're not married?" he asked, knowing the answer.

"Widowed. My husband died eight years ago in a trucking accident."

"I'm sorry. Kids?"

"My daughter, Erin, who used to work some at the shop on the weekends, just graduated from high school and is attending TU this fall. You?"

"I have two in high school and they live in Tulsa with their mom. I get to see them on the weekends some." He pulled the pickup into the auto parts parking lot.

"Can you put this on the tester for me?" Brent placed the battery on the counter and spoke to the young man behind the counter.

Alice walked to the vending machine in the corner

while they waited and returned with two drinks handing him one. "It's the least I can do. You've been so kind."

As Brent popped the top on the soda, the clerk returned without the battery. "It's toast, man. I've got some in the back that should fit. You want one?"

Brent raised an eyebrow at Alice and she nodded.

The new battery installed, Brent turned to Alice. "It's getting late and I wondered if you would like a pizza or something?" He smiled his best smile thinking he might be finally winning her over—at least as a friend.

"I really need to get home. Erin will be coming in and expect something for dinner. She's been at the office all day in Tulsa."

"Well, then we'll take it to your house and eat it there. I don't really know your daughter. I've seen her a few times on the weekends."

Alice thought about the man in front of her and then smiled. "Okay, but only if you let me buy. You've done enough already."

With the pizza on the counter top of the small kitchen, Alice took plates from the cabinet and set out a pitcher of tea. "I hope you like tea. I don't have much else to drink now. I work in a grocery store and hate to go grocery shopping."

"Tea is fine." Brent inspected the small, neat house with pictures on the wall of the young girl he knew only as Erin, the weekend flower shop worker who recently quit. She could be a twin to her mother only with dark hair and eyes. He had seen her on the floor working, but never spoken to her other than to say hi.

"So, how often do you see your kids?" Alice placed the large iced tea glasses on the table and gestured for Brent to sit.

"Normally every other weekend, but as they get older they have activities. I managed to see them more when I lived in Tulsa. I hoped to have them over soon for a camping trip out by the lake. Can you recommend a good camping place?"

"Well, there are a couple of places we used to go. I really don't camp much anymore, but Erin and her friends do. They know the good places. Alice took a bite of pizza and wiped her mouth with a napkin just as the back door slammed and Erin's voice rang out.

"Mom?"

"In the kitchen hon."

Erin walked in the kitchen in a black skirt and top she had taken from her aunt's house a few weeks ago. Appearing older than the young girl normally in cut-offs and flip flops she stopped and stared at Brent—and then her mom. Brent rose.

"Erin, you know Brent Taylor, the manager at the store."

Erin nodded. "Mr. Taylor," she murmured.

"My car died in the parking lot after work. Dead battery. Brent was kind enough to help me out, so I bought dinner to thank him. How was work?"

Erin continued to stare at the man in her kitchen. "Um fine. Still doing grunt work on that case."

"Erin is working as a clerk in a law firm that my sister is a partner in. She is very lucky and loves the work. She is working full time for another week and then part time this fall as she takes classes at TU."

"Congratulations, Erin. It's a big step from a flower shop to a law office, I'd think." Brent folded his napkin, the tension in the room thick enough to cut with a knife.

"I like it. But it takes a little getting used to." Erin stood silent.

"Well, I need to get going," Brent said shoving the last bite in his mouth and taking his plate to the sink. "Alice, thank you for dinner and I hope the battery is the end of your car troubles."

"You don't have to leave. You've only had one piece."

"No, you don't have to leave," Erin said. "I'm going to change. Excuse me." She walked from the room down the hall to her bedroom.

"I'm sorry, Alice. That seemed a little awkward. I'll get out of your hair and you can visit with your daughter."

"Really you don't have to go. But at least take some home with you. Erin and I will never eat all this." She placed two pieces of pizza on a paper plate and covered them with foil handing them to Brent.

"Thanks again for dinner but I need to be going." He took the paper plate from her hands.

"I should be thanking you or I might still be in that parking lot." Alice held the door open for Brent to leave.

Brent walked out the door with pizza in hand just as Alice's phone rang. The screen read 'Felicity.'

"Hi lady, how goes it?" she asked her best friend. "What's wrong, are you crying? He what? Get over here. I have pizza and we need to talk. Well, bring your toothbrush. You can stay here tonight. That's what friends are for." She clicked off and glanced up as her daughter walked in the door dressed more like the little girl she had raised.

"Everything okay?" Erin asked.

"Well no. Felicity says Frank wants a divorce. She's coming over. I'm not surprised really. Things have been tough between them for some time.

"Erin, Mr. Taylor just helped me out this evening. It is nothing more than that." Alice cleared the table.

"I know Mom. But it would be okay if it was more than that."

"Well, it isn't. But you seemed a little surprised when you walked in and I just wanted you to know."

"I'm a little surprised, but it's your life after all." Erin took a plate down and put pizza on it.

"He just helped me out."

"Okay. But what about Felicity?"

"I guess that jerk-of-a-husband of hers has a girlfriend. It has been going on for a while and now he wants out of the marriage." Alice wiped the crumbs from the table.

"That's awful. Well, she's better off without him then, if he is cheating."

"Maybe. Life is complicated. Things are going to be tough for her and the boys now. Anyway, she is coming over and probably spending the night. The kids went to Grandma's one last time before school starts."

"Well, hide the Margaritas." Erin smiled as she bit into the slice of pizza.

"I think she learned her lesson last time. Anyway, all I have is tea. I think there's salad from last night too if you want to get it out. It's Friday night. You kids doing anything?" Alice walked to the refrigerator and opened it.

"I don't know. Bernadette and Steve are really getting thick these days. I hardly ever see her."

"Yeah, I've noticed that Rob is getting very attentive. Are you two getting close? I mean is there a change in your relationship?" Alice sat back down placing the salad bowl on the kitchen table.

"I don't know. I know he wants to, but somehow it is just too weird having one of your best friends turn into your boyfriend."

"Well he's a good guy and I know you'll make the right decision."

Alice rose to the sound of the knock at the kitchen door and opened it to a tear stained face. Felicity stood blowing her nose. "You have any more tissues? I've already been through a box I think."

"I've got lots and besides, I work at a grocery store if we need more." Alice hugged her long-time friend tightly and the sobs began again.

Chapter 12

Erin pounded the last tent stake into the dried-out ground with a claw hammer from her dad's garage. Even though he had been gone for eight years, she would always think of it as Dad's garage. The tent sat at a slight angle with the door facing the downhill slope to the water. With the windows unzipped and flaps tied back, she should get most of the water-cooled breeze as the sun set. She tried her best to be sure there were no rocks under the tent floor. She learned at an early age rocks were never welcome under a sleeping bag poking her in the back. It might be the last time Erin and her best friends could camp before school started.

"Want to hike down to the water?" Erin tossed the hammer in the tent. Camping, a part of Erin's childhood she always held close to her heart. She loved her friend and the lake where they grew up. Camping with her was like icing on the cake.

"Sure, let's do it. The guys won't be here for a while." Bernadette headed for the trail head.

They followed the shore along a path they took many times when they were younger. They knew the shoreline even though it changed often with storms and lake levels. But today it reminded Erin of the days when they were children. They weren't children anymore and they weren't exactly adults yet either.

"Augggg! I lost my flip flop!" Bernadette stood

knee deep in sinking sand. She plopped down on the soggy sand, her butt sinking, and felt around. They called it quickie sand even though you could find the bottom. Not like in the Tarzan movie where the person quickly sank to their neck, but the sand still felt soggy and pulled off her shoe. "Wait, I feel something with my toe."

Erin walked back to her friend in the mud just as she triumphantly pulled the caked sandal from the muck and stood giggling. She reached for Erin's hand with her own covered in wet sand and her best friend pulled her up on the bank to safer ground. The sand sucked one last time at her foot as she pulled it to freedom.

"Well, that was gross," Bernadette said brushing off the wet, crusted sand from her legs and then walked out into the lake to finish the job.

"We haven't found that stuff in years, it's been so dry, I can't believe that it's still there," Erin said standing next to her in the sun. Evening light filtered through the lacy tree leaves. It was Erin's favorite time of day on the water when the waves became glass and the shad jumped in the diamond sprinkled water. She could live her life like this, she thought watching the ripples as the afternoon slowed to evening.

"I wonder how many people have not spent an afternoon like this next to the water?" Erin watched as a shad jumped in front of her and several more followed. Something larger followed under the water and the fish led its school to safety.

"I don't know, but I think we were lucky to grow up here. It might not be as glamorous as some places, but the water sooths your soul." Bernadette contemplated the water where the shad still flopped.

"We'd better head back before the guys get here. I'm starving." Erin gazed at the water with her hand up, keeping the sun from her eyes. She breathed deeply one last time.

"Burgers, yum!" Bernadette said putting on her rinsed flip flops. They took a different route back avoiding the swampy mess this time.

The hike conjured up the ghost of a lifelong friendship between the girls. Bernadette and Erin always told each other everything. At least until now. Erin had to remain silent about things she learned at the firm. The first rule in a law office. And because of that, sometimes she felt she and her best friend were drifting apart.

Bernadette sat on the picnic table hooking up the speaker for her iPhone when the boys drove up in Rob's pickup. The last weekend before classes started on Monday and Erin secured a camping place with a table and a grill. The guys were bringing the burgers and chips.

"Prime location, ladies." Steve jumped out of the pickup and reached in the back for the ice chest. "And I just happen to have USDA Prime Angus burger meat—straight from my grandpa's ranch—for your dining pleasure."

"Ohh, nothing but the best!" Bernadette hopped up from the table where she sat in her damp shorts. She walked to Steve and kissed him lightly on the lips then grabbed one end of the ice chest lifting it onto the concrete picnic table. The Corp of Engineers placed the behemoth monstrosities everywhere around the lake for use by campers, making them heavy enough no one could steal them, and they became a permanent part of the landscape.

"I also managed to secure a few brewskies from Grandpa's frig for later." Steve spoke with a smile on his face.

"Better keep those under wraps for now. The Lake Patrol has been running around here and we don't need anyone thinking there's underage drinking going on." Bernadette lifted the bag of half-pound burger patties out of the ice. "These do look good. I guess Grandpa knows we're eating his cows?"

"Of course. He suggested I come over and get them. I kinda snuck the beer though."

"Well, I have the charcoal. All the Angus burger in the world is nothing without a good bed of hot coals." Rob dumped charcoal briquettes into the aging barbeque pit and stacked them into a cone.

"Just like a Boy Scout," Erin said with a grin.

"Be prepared, I always say." He grinned back then eyed his friend who stood with his arm around Bernadette. "Steve, you got the lighter fluid and matches?"

"No, I thought you had them."

"Why would I have them? You said you were the king of the grill and I was to bring the charcoal. How are we going to light this thing?"

Steve shrugged.

"Well, you said you were a Boy Scout." Erin stood beside the grill surveying the cold charcoal. "Ever make a fire without matches?"

Rob grumbled something under his breath as he walked away picking up sticks and grass along the way. Dry grass stuck out from the landscape in the hot Oklahoma sun everywhere this time of year.

Bernadette sighed. "Okay, I'm going to the store." She walked toward the jeep pulling her keys from her pocket.

"I wonder if that family up the hill has matches we can borrow." Steve walked away leaving Erin staring into the cold pit with the cone shaped pile of useless charcoal. She felt bad for Rob. Maybe she should not tease him so much.

"I know you're trying hard, but really, who doesn't remember matches and lighter fluid for a cook out?" Erin shook her head and took a step back.

She could feel Rob's eyes boring into her back when he returned with his hands full of grass, twigs, and bark. He piled the bark and grass into the opposite end of the barbeque pit where he first made the pyramid of black coal. Fashioning it into a nest he began the spindling motion with the stick trying to make enough friction to get a spark.

"Erin, will you please quit hovering like that. It is not making this any easier." Rob gently pushed her aside with his elbow.

"Sorry," she said walking away to the ice chest and popping the top off a can of soda. "You want one?" Rob only shook his head.

Erin unfolded two chairs by the tent, then plopped down watching Rob in his endless quest for fire. She had long ago lost track of Steve as he traipsed from camper to camper asking for matches. She had no idea where he went. She leaned back in the chair staring up into the ever-darkening evening sky when the pop of a twig snapped her back to reality. Had he done it? Built a fire?

"Will this help?" A Lake Patrol trooper stood next

to Rob with a long handled lighter—the blue flame stretching out the end and lighting the grass at the base of the fire nest.

"Thanks man," Rob said with a broad smile. "We might have been here all night. Someone forgot the matches."

The officer smiled in return. "Been there."

The lights of the Jeep pulled in beside the tent just as Steve came running up breathless. "I found some." He held out his hand to show three slightly damp and bent matches in his wet palm.

"Got some!" Bernadette said stepping out of the car and walking up to the grill where everyone crowded over the brightly blazing fire. Rob transferred the blazing grass to the pile of charcoal.

"There'll be burgers soon. Get your mouths ready." Rob smiled glancing back over his shoulder at Erin.

"You got that started without matches?" Bernadette and Steve stared at the charcoal grill.

"Not sayin' I did, not sayin' I didn't. But I am an engineering major." Rob folded his arms over his chest and viewed his accomplishment.

"You kids have a safe night now," said the trooper as he walked away holding the lighter close to his body and out of sight. "At least I know now you won't starve."

"Thanks, Officer," Rob said.

All four campers were soon wiping juice from their chins. The only noise in the darkening evening was the sound of chewing and groans.

"Rob these taste like the burgers my dad used to make." Erin wiped her mouth once more. She often related food to good times with friends. Dad's burgers were the best. He made them on the grill he received for Father's Day, and that grill still sat in her backyard. Tonight, with friends and burgers—that almost didn't happen—again she would remember her friends and the food they ate that night.

"Oh, I don't think I can eat another bite. These are probably the best burgers I have ever eaten." Bernadette put the last of her hamburger back on the paper plate with the chips.

"Really, guys. The best." Erin gathered her paper plate and napkin and began to stand to throw away the leftovers.

"You're not throwing that out?" Steve reached over and took the small piece of meat and bun still on the plate and popped it in his mouth.

"Well, I guess not."

"Here you can have mine too." Bernadette held the last of her burger up in front of Steve's mouth, and he playfully snatched it with his teeth.

"A human garbage disposal," Bernadette said with a smile. "I'm so full. Let's go for a walk." She held out her hand to Steve and they walked off into the camp ground hand in hand.

"That's okay. I'll put up the tent in the dark by myself after cooking your dinner. Don't worry about a thing!" Rob called out to Steve as they left. Steve lifted one hand in a wave without ever looking back.

The full moon rose over the opposite side of the lake as Erin cleaned up the trash and put the leftovers into the ice chest. Then she helped Rob pull the tent upright. It leaned slightly to the left on a bent frame but couldn't be helped. He quickly tossed the rolled-up sleeping bags into the tent and walked away.

"Have a seat." Erin patted the chair next to her and Rob folded his long legs into a seated position, staring out into the water. The gently lapping waves joined the tree frogs in a serenade. Clouds were forming in the distance.

"Next week is the big one." Erin said never taking her eyes off the giant harvest moon as it rose, clouds rolling across its face.

"Yeah, you ready?" Rob wiggled trying to get comfortable in a chair too small for him.

"As I'll ever be, I guess. I have classes Monday, Wednesday, and Friday and work the other two days. I guess I'll study in between." Erin drained the last of the soda.

"Yeah, me too. I have class three days and the work schedule varies. Sometimes I work in the library until they close at nine. But it is easy work. Just putting books back and stuff. I can study when I'm not busy."

Giggles were heard as Bernadette and Steve made their way back to the camp site. They quickly walked to the ice chest and pulled out two beers laughing and whispering in each other's ears.

"Good night all," Steve said as they made their way to the boy's tent.

"Hey, that's my tent. I put it up." Rob spoke to his friend as he walked into the leaning tent.

"Thanks, bro!" Steve held the tent flap open for Bernadette and winked at his friends.

Erin watched in amazement as Bernadette climbed into the tent zipping it closed, and then the giggles began in earnest.

"When did they become a couple?" Erin stared after her long-time friend.

"This summer while you were working."

"Have I really been that blind? I mean I didn't work that much and I still saw you guys."

"You've been pretty busy this summer. We almost never saw you." Rob reached for a soda and popped the top, draining most of it in one gulp, belching loudly.

"Well, in school we saw each other every day and now we don't, but we still talked and stuff."

Rob leaned over the ice chest again. "You want one?" He stood up with a beer in his hand.

"No. Well maybe. I probably won't drink it all. Maybe we should get in the tent with that in case the trooper comes back."

"After you." Rob gestured to the tent flap. "I think it is going to rain anyway," he said as the drizzle began.

Erin hesitated.

"I can sleep in the truck if you would rather."

"No of course not. You can have my sleeping bag. I'm sure Bernadette's pink kid-sized bag will be too short for you."

"And not do anything good for my masculinity," Rob said smiling.

Once inside the tight quarters, Erin could hear the sizzle of rain as it spattered on the still hot barbeque grill. They climbed in the tent just in time. Rob stepped back out closing the windows and pulling the ice chest next to the door. He handed Erin the bag with the chips.

"Soggy chips are awful. Besides, chips go good with beer."

"I don't know how you can be hungry after all we ate." She sat next to the pink sleeping bag.

"Not hungry, just have the munchies." He opened the chip bag.

"My dad always drank this brand of beer. I don't mean he drank all the time, just when he did, he drank this brand." Erin held the bottle up to the moonlight coming in through the slit left open by the covering for the windows.

"Last time I saw my old man he was drinkin'," Rob said with a swallow.

"I don't know anything about your family. You never talked about them," Erin said as she unrolled the child-sized sleeping bag. Too warm to climb inside, she knew her legs would be doubled up if she did. She let her feet hang off then end. She lay back and eyed the tent. "You know if you don't touch the inside of the tent, it will keep us dry, right."

"I learned that much in Boy Scouts. Obviously, you've camped some. You can pitch a tent by yourself."

"We used to camp as a family. Dad and I would fish, and Mom would just sit on the bank and read or something." Erin kicked off her shoes.

"Must have been nice. My dad ran off about the same time as yours died, I guess. Mom just worked all the time trying to make ends meet. We never did much as a family."

"What does your mom do?" Erin took another drink of the beer that tasted good after all.

"She works for the county. She is in the Assessor's office."

"Oh, I'm in and out of the courthouse all the time. I should introduce myself."

"She's the grumpy gray-haired lady—well, there's more than one of them. She never got over Dad's leaving."

"It's hard to do. Mom never got over Dad either, I don't think. Not that the situations are the same, but she never dated or anything. However, I did come home the other night and she and the store manager, Brent Taylor, were eating pizza in our kitchen. Her car battery died. He helped her out. She said she repaid him with pizza. He seemed nervous and left once I showed up. Understandable I guess, since I just stood there with my mouth open. But, weird. Mom with a man." She wiped her mouth with the back of her hand.

"Well, now that you are growing up and leaving home, maybe she thinks she will be lonely." He reached for another chip.

"Yeah, I hate that. It's the biggest reason I didn't go into the dorms this year. I didn't like leaving her alone."

"Or maybe she would like a little alone time." Rob munched the chips noisily.

"I doubt it. But maybe she has been waiting for me to leave before she got on with her life."

Thunder boomed, and the tent lit up from the lightning in the distance. Erin could see Rob sitting cross legged on her sleeping bag with the bag of chips in his hand. He offered her one.

"No thanks. Still full."

"Well, this is our first night together and I'm eating chips and you're laying over there."

"Sorry, not hungry." She rolled over and scrutinized Rob.

"You're avoiding the subject." He stared at her on the opposite side of the tent.

"We talked about this, and I thought we decided to just be friends."

"We talked about it, and *you* decided to just be friends. That doesn't mean I won't keep trying, Erin."

"I'm not having sex with you, Rob, just because the neighbors are. That is not what this weekend is about." Erin pulled back the top of the sleeping bag.

"I know. I'm just putting it out there. You know, in case you change your mind in the night or something." He reached in for another chip.

"I'll let you know. And don't get greasy chips all over my sleeping bag." She rolled over and curled up on the too-short sleeping bag yawning deeply. She didn't need a boyfriend in her life yet. The rain spattered on the outside of the tent and a cool breeze blew in around the tent window flap. Munching could be heard across the tent from a teenaged boy who never filled up. Erin fell asleep almost instantly and slept like the little girl who used to camp with her parents in the cozy tent listening to the rain.

## Chapter 13

Before school started Erin and Bernadette planned to find the buildings on their schedules and get an idea of how far they were from available parking and the trolley that circled the campus. But the plan fell short of becoming a reality. When Monday morning arrived, Erin looked like every other freshman on campus with a class schedule in one hand and a campus map in the other.

She circled the parking lot several times and finally found a parking spot—still a long way from her destination. She hoisted the backpack up again and stared at the tower in the distance which should be her destination. She'd barely make it in time.

With classes on Monday, Wednesday, and Friday she would have time for full days at the law firm twice a week and she knew she would need it. They loaded her up sometimes. No one went to the courthouse unless they had to—they waited on Erin to do the document filing. She found herself running up and down the block to the brick building, sometimes morning and afternoon, to get the precious file stamp with the correct date on it—sometimes just as the doors were about to close.

But today she had classes. Erin's class schedule, marked "Pre-Law" at the top, stated a major. That set her apart from most freshmen, who were still undecided. Erin knew she had to take the LSAT her junior year, but it never occurred to her that she wouldn't get in to law school. The universe just would not do that to someone who always wanted to be a lawyer, would it?

Opening the door to the huge auditorium she glanced around for Bernadette. In a sea of undergraduates, she needed to find her friends. Students were seated in chairs, some with their books strewn over more than one desk, feet on the backs of others. Erin walked down the steps toward the bottom of the lecture hall.

"Hey, girlfriend." Bernadette tapped her on the shoulder. "We're over here." She pointed and then bounced up two steps and slid down the aisle where Rob and Steve sat with their books out. Rob smiled and tapped his book with a pencil then cleared a place for her to sit. Bernadette climbed over Steve's long legs to her chair. As Erin sat, the professor knocked on the microphone. Erin almost always ran late.

"Studying at my place tonight," Bernadette whispered over the two boys that sat between them. Erin nodded, and the lecture began.

Classes filled much of the morning and Bernadette and Erin ran to the cafeteria for a sandwich at noon. Finally, some time together.

"So, you are working in the Sociology department? What days?" Erin set her tray down eyeing Bernadette across the table.

"Only twenty hours a week—that is all that work study will allow—but they move me around from professor to professor doing menial jobs and I only find out the week prior what days I'll work. They have to work around my class schedule though."

"Do you like it?" Erin poured the catsup on her fries.

"It's okay. There is this one secretary that must be a hundred years old and she is such a pain. 'Bernadette, do this. Bernadette, do that. What took you so long? And it's not right.' She's ridiculous and nobody wants to work for her. But one of the young professors took pity on me the other day and had me doing stuff for him my whole shift. I wish I could work for him all the time."

"What kind of things do you do?" Erin tasted the limp fries and decided on the salad.

"Oh, you know, copying, filing, making coffee, whatever they want."

"Kinda sounds like my job."

"Yeah, but you're learning something you'll use. I'm just doing grunt work nobody else wants to do." Bernadette folded the napkin in her lap.

"Believe me, I know what that's like too. Anyway, I never see you anymore. We need a girl's night." Erin hoped for a chance to talk to Bernadette about Steve, but the crowded cafeteria made it difficult for that conversation.

"You mean like clubbing? Or painting our nails?"

"You know I don't go clubbing and neither do you."

"I know, just checking to see if you had changed, since the last time we got together."

"It hasn't been that long." Erin shoved a bit of sandwich in her mouth.

Bernadette smiled her mischievous smile. "I'm just hassling you."

Erin wiped her mouth and swallowed the bite of sandwich. "So, you and Steve are an item?"'

Bernadette nodded. "Weird huh? I mean I hadn't planned on coupling off this soon into college, but he is so adorable, I just can't not see him! That's really weird when you think about how I hated him in grade school for stealing my tricycle."

"Well, people change. Besides, he probably stole your tricycle to get to talk to you. He's probably been smitten with you forever."

"I doubt it. He was a little turkey when he was young."

Erin stood with her tray. "I gotta run. I get out of class at 4:00. Want to study then?"

"Sure. Four fifteen in my room. See you then." Bernadette grabbed her tray and ran for the door.

****

Another grueling day at the firm running errands for everyone and at 4:00 Nathan needed a slew of documents copied, filed, and mailed to opposing counsel. If Erin had to guess, he did it on purpose. Still angry at her about the incident in the board room. His assistant, Janice, was always friendly enough, but Nathan acted aloof and distant. In fact, he didn't speak to her at all. He sent Janice to do the talking.

"Three sets file-stamped?"

"Yes. And mail a copy to opposing counsel. His name and address are at the bottom." Janice stood in her skirt and blouse, no shoes, no jacket, and her hair in her eyes. Evidently Nathan had been working her to the bone as well. Erin knew she had a jacket when she came in that probably hung on the back of her chair. The shoes she wore to work that day, kicked off under the desk. Nathan worked the woman to death—probably why she was rail thin.

Papers stuffed in the briefcase, that stayed at the Reception desk for everyone's use, Erin ran to the courthouse and grabbed the elevator door about to close. Down the hall, she yanked open the door that read "Judge Hardridge." His bailiff, Nicole, sat behind the desk in charge of his docket and his life at work. Young and pretty, with dark hair and eyes that were now red, she sniffed wiping her nose and then smiled at Erin when she walked in.

"They sending you on another wild goose chase today?" Nicole reached for another tissue.

"Always. Is the judge in? I need a signature on an Order."

"No, he's gone home. But I can keep it for his signature in the morning."

Erin tapped her foot impatiently. "Well, I guess there's no other way. I'll let Janice know it's over here and she can pick it up in the morning or something. Are you okay? Have you been crying?"

"No, I'm fine." Nicole dabbed at her eyes.

"You sure?" Erin studied the bailiff.

"I'm good." The pregnant pause hung between them with urgency. "Just ran into a jerk, you know?" Nicole replied.

"Yes, there are plenty of them out there. You sure you're fine?"

"Yes." She paused then shook her head. "I mean no." She sniffed and wiped her nose again and then hesitated once more. "Can I confide in you?"

Erin barely knew this girl, but she seemed so fragile and needed a friend. "Of course. Everything okay?"

"Not really. I guess I'm just being silly. I went out with this jerk last night. I didn't realize he was such a jerk. I saw him as cute and seemed nice enough at first, and then once we were alone, a different story."

"Yes, I know the type." This was about to get personal.

"I know we don't know each other very well. I hope you don't think I'm an idiot, but—well…"

The courthouse closed within minutes. Thankfully she left the papers at the court clerk's office to be file-stamped today before running to the judge's office. But she still had to pick them back up. Erin made herself not bounce back and forth on her feet waiting on the story. She reminded herself to be still, this woman needed someone to talk to.

"Of course not. You're fine. Did something happen?" Erin really didn't have time to listen to this woman's romantic encounters.

"He tried to rape me!" She burst into tears.

Now Erin felt worse than ever about wanting to leave. If she were the woman behind the desk she would need someone to talk to. "Oh, honey! Did you tell someone? I mean you are bringing charges, right? This is a crime."

"Noooooo. I can't do that."

"Why not?"

"You don't know him or his family. Or maybe you do. They are a very prominent family and I would be causing them trouble."

"Okay, were you hurt? I mean physically?"

"No. Well my blouse was torn, and I walked home in heels. My feet are sore, and I got almost no sleep last night. Erin, I thought he wouldn't stop."

"I don't know what to tell you. I might feel the same way if I were you, but you really need to tell someone in authority. What if it happens again?" Erin leaned in and patted the woman's hand.

The door banged open and a young man with a friendly face walked in. "Hey Nicole. Dad in?"

Nicole wiped her nose and quickly put on her sunglasses picking up papers and straightening her desk.

"No, Jake, the judge left hours ago after his last docket and I'm about to."

"Oh, okay. I didn't mean to intrude. Everything okay?" The tall thin boy with red hair and freckles smiled pleasantly.

"Yes. Jake this is Erin, she works for Cronkite and Associates."

"Hi, Erin." He reached out his hand and she shook it quickly. "Okay, thanks, I'll catch up with him at home. I can see you need to get going. We'll talk later." The tall, lanky young man left the office without another word.

"The judge's son."

"Yes, I gathered."

"He's a good guy, like his dad. Erin, I'm sorry I dumped on you. I can't believe I went out with him in the first place."

"Nicole, it is not your fault. You went out with him because you didn't know what he was like. It's not your fault."

"I was stupid." She gathered her purse and turned off lights. The courthouse hours ended, and Erin did not have all the documents to take back to the office.

"No, you weren't. Come on we'll walk out together. Does the courthouse open at 8:30 in the morning? I need to pick up the papers at the court clerk."

"Yeah, 8:30 to 5:00. I'm sorry I made you late. I'll ask the judge to sign the Order as soon as he gets in tomorrow."

Erin and Nicole walked down the hall and waited for the elevator. How would she tell Janice about the documents she did not get picked up? Maybe she could swing by the courthouse at 8:30 in the morning on the way to class and then drop them off at the office with Janice. Maybe.

Running up the stairs and yanking the door open to the office she found it quiet. Ordinarily there were people there at all hours. Today, everyone left on time. Stephanie emerged from the back with her purse in hand and nodded slightly on her way out the door. Erin had to find Janice and tell her she didn't have the documents with her. She walked down the hall listening for someone still in the office and came to Janice's cubicle. She had already closed for the day. Erin searched for a pad and pen on the immaculate desk and found nothing. Finally, she pulled paper from the copier and wrote her a note stating she would be by first thing in the morning to complete her task. Then left for home.

Chapter 14

"Hey, Mom, I'm home!" Erin called to her mother as she came in the back door of the house. No answer.

"Mom?"

"In here!" Her mother's voice came from her bedroom.

Erin walked down the hall lined with pictures of her as she grew up. At the end of the hall hung the latest one of her in her cap and gown; on the opposite wall were family pictures of her and her parents in younger days.

Her mother's door slightly ajar, Erin peeked in. Her mother stood in the middle of the room wearing only a slip. Several dresses were hung on the dresser knobs and some lay across the bed. "I'm glad you're here. I need your help."

"What's up? Going somewhere?" Erin's mother never went anywhere except work.

"I need you to tell me which of these dresses looks best on me."

"What's the occasion?" Erin walked toward the bed where the clothes lay.

"Nothing special just going out to dinner with a friend." Her mother fidgeted nervously.

"You're going out? You? Where ya going?"

"Erin," her mother stammered and then walked toward her. "I should have talked to you earlier, but I don't see you as much as I used to. Um, I'm going to have dinner with Brent. Nothing special, just as friends." She paused watching her daughter. "Do you think that is okay?"

"Brent Taylor? Your boss?"

"Well, technically he is the manager of the store, but I manage the flower shop which is essentially a store of its own, not just a department, like the others."

"Of course, I didn't mean that. Just making sure I knew who you meant." In all the time Alice had been her mother, she was just Mom, not someone who went out. Especially on a date. She remembered a girl in middle school whose mother dated, and the girl talked about waking up with someone new in the house all the time. Erin knew Mom wouldn't do that. Dating! Weird.

Alice stood with her arms folded over her chest. "Erin if this is not okay with you…"

"No, Mom, it's fine. Just a little confusing, that's all. I mean you have never done this. Is it because of me? Did you not date all this time because you had me in the house?"

"No, of course not. I just never found anyone I wanted to go out with, I guess."

"So, he's the one?" Erin picked up a blouse looking it over.

"No. Just a friend. I'm not trying to replace your father, surely you know that. I couldn't even if I tried." A tear welled up in her eye and then rolled down her cheek. She quickly brushed it away.

Oh, way to go Erin, make her cry. "Mom, I'm sorry. I didn't mean to make you cry. You'll ruin your makeup."

Her mom sniffed. "I know you loved your dad. I

103

loved him too, but he is gone and there is nothing either of us can do about that."

After Erin's father's truck slid off the road rolling down the hill on a Rocky Mountain highway, the trucking company brought a fruit basket—aware Alice owned the only flower shop in the tiny town. They said her father died instantly of his wounds and didn't suffer. Erin wondered. They thought he might have swerved to miss a deer—that sounded like him—when he lost control on the icy curve and took out the guard rail on the way over. Erin and Alice never visited the scene of the accident. But, Erin had a picture in her mind of the Rockies in all their winter splendor and she refused to see the blood that accompanied it.

"Dad was my hero. I remember playing catch with him in the front yard, like the son he never had, while you cooked dinner. I spent a lot of hours in the garage with him as he overhauled that '57 Chevy. I still think of him whenever I smell grease and oil. A garage still conjures up memories of Dad and the hours we spent together when he wasn't on the road."

"He loved you too, sweetie." Her mom sniffed then blew her nose and then hugged her daughter.

"Help me with these dresses, will you please? What about the pink one?"

Erin wiped her eyes. Experience taught her that crying would not fix this problem. "No, that's like Sunday morning. You need more like Saturday night."

"It's Tuesday."

"I know. Where you going anyway?"

"I'm not sure. I don't know what he likes to eat besides donuts at a meeting and the pizza I brought home the night he helped me with the car."

"Ah, a health nut. Okay, now we're getting somewhere. How about that black one?"

"No, too slinky and a little low cut. Maybe the floral?" Alice gestured toward the dresser where a dress hung on a hanger.

"Yea, that one will blend with the blue earrings you're wearing."

The doorbell rang, and Erin peeked at her mother. "Get dressed, I'll get it."

Erin opened the door to a smiling Brent Taylor whose smile faded when he saw her. Maybe he expected to be alone with her mother. Or did he not like her?

"Hi Erin. I wasn't expecting you." He stood with a box of candy. Smart enough not to bring flowers to the woman who managed his flower shop. One point for him.

"Mr. Taylor. Come in. Mom's almost ready."

Brent walked in to the small living room and handed the box of chocolates to Erin. "You look hungry. Want to join us tonight? It's all you can eat catfish at the Fish-N-Go."

"Whoa, nothing but the best."

"Does your mom like fish, I never asked."

"As long as she doesn't have to catch it or clean it. Come in and have a seat." She pointed him to the sofa.

Brent sat uncomfortably on the edge of the couch. "So, how's the law office? They working you hard? Your mom talks about that new job of yours all the time."

"Grunt work, but I stay busy."

"Well, really, do you want to join us for dinner?" Brent asked apologetically.

Erin knew a pity gesture when she saw one. Poor young girl left all alone while her mother ran around.

"No thanks. I have a lot of studying to do."

"Well if you're sure."

Alice walked in the door of the living room in the floral dress and flats. Erin saw she didn't try to dress up the outfit with heels, especially since Brent wore jeans.

"Evening, Brent."

Brent stood and walked her way reaching for her hand and then put it back in his pocket.

"Alice, you look lovely. I tried to get this young lady to join us tonight, but she says she has homework."

"Honey, you sure?"

"No thanks, Mom. You go have fun. I'll make a sandwich."

"There's left over casserole in the frig if you want to nuke it."

"Okay, thanks. I'll find something." Erin hoped they left soon so she wouldn't feel so uncomfortable.

"Okay. Well, I'm ready if you are, Brent." Alice appeared nervous as she snuck a peek at her daughter and they left through the front door. "Good night hon."

"Night, Mom, Mr. Taylor. Have fun." Erin thought she sounded like the parent this time.

She kicked off her shoes and padded into the kitchen for leftovers, but not before she turned on the TV. Life—always changing.

Chapter 15

Erin ran out the door with her backpack in hand and threw it into the passenger side of the car. She planned to leave at least five minutes earlier but could not get everything together. She fell asleep on the couch last night studying and her mom woke her when she tiptoed in.

She wanted to be at the courthouse at 8:30 when they opened so she could grab the documents, drop them off with Janice, and still make it to class on time. Now it might not happen if she ran into traffic.

Screeching to a halt, she parked the car and ran for the courthouse sliding into the crowded elevator just before it closed. She hoped Nicole got the judge's signature as soon as he came in. Assuming the judge made it on time this morning. Pulling open the door to his office she found Nicole behind the desk and on the phone. Good, she wouldn't have to talk to her again. She needed to be at school on time. Nicole smiled and handed the signed documents over the counter as she chattered on the line to someone else. Erin smiled and waved, then ran for the court clerk's office.

Erin slid in the door of Cronkite and Associates just as Janice walked up the steps in heels juggling a briefcase and commuter cup.

"Janice. I have those documents file-stamped that you gave me last night. By the time I got back to the court clerk's they were closed. I left you a note." Erin breathed heavily after climbing the stairs.

"Oh, thank you. You really didn't have to come back this morning. I know you have class. I would have picked them up."

"Well, I wanted to finish what I started." Erin moved back down the stairs as she spoke.

"Well thanks again. See you tomorrow." Janice walked down the hall to her office carrying the brief case, load of documents, and balancing the cup of coffee on top. The woman kept so many balls in the air, any amount Nathan paid her was not enough.

Back in the parking lot, Erin turned and ran for the car.

She took a deep breath before opening the door to the lecture hall knowing that class had already started and found her friends in their usual place saving a spot for her. She made it. She accomplished everything she needed. She smiled at Rob, his green eyes crinkling in the corners, and marveled at the way they sparkled even in the dim light of the lecture hall.

Then it hit her. She accomplished almost everything she set out to do that morning. Except for picking up the book she left at the office yesterday. Damn! She needed that text to study tonight and didn't want to have to go back to the office again today. She settled into the seat and opened her texts.

The day dragged on—one class after another and Erin and Bernadette made plans to study after classes. She wondered sometimes why she went back home at night. It would be so much easier, and quicker, to stay in Tulsa. She had work and school here. But she knew why. Her mom needed her. Or did she? She was dating!

Still too weird to think about. She couldn't remember the last time they ate dinner together. Their schedules took them different ways.

"I really need that Poly Sci book I left at the office. I took it the other day to study during lunch and then hardly got to even glance at it."

"You want me to go with you?" Bernadette, in her sweats and socks, sat on her bed with the covers over her. She thought she felt a cold coming on. Her curls were tied back with a clip to control them as she thumbed through book after book that surrounded her.

"I really don't want to go. It's late, you're sick, and I need to go home. I probably wouldn't get any studying done anyway. I waste a lot of time running back and forth not to mention gas."

"Well maybe you should think about moving into the dorms next semester."

"Maybe. I stayed at home for Mom. But did you know she is dating someone?"

"Yeah, you said. Is that okay with you?" Bernadette sniffed and pulled another tissue from the box.

"Well, yeah, I mean it is her life."

"True. And she's never said anything about you not dating." She blew her nose and tossed the used tissue into the trash next to the bed.

"Oh, like I ever have a date!" Erin snorted.

"Well, if you did." Bernadette's phone buzzed, and she smiled. The caller ID read Steve.

Erin picked up her books and loaded them into the ever-enlarging backpack. Eventually it would reach a breaking point. She waved goodbye to her best friend and left her to talk privately to her boyfriend. Studying was obviously over for the evening.

Leaving the parking lot, Erin paused. It wasn't that far to the office and she really needed that book. She turned the car in the direction of Cronkite and Associates.

Shadows at the back door appeared dark and creepy, but there were still cars in the parking lot, so someone worked late. One car belonged to N. Robert Cronkite. Her footsteps echoed in the strangely quiet halls of the firm as she made her way to the cubicle she called home two days a week.

"Lose something?" Robert Cronkite stood at the end of the hall backlit by the emergency lights near the floor. His white hair—always in need of a trim—stuck out from the sides of his head as he ran his fingers through it. His shirttail out on one side.

"Sorry sir. I didn't mean to disturb you. I left a book here and thought I'd pick it up on the way home. I was on campus."

He shuffled her way and stood in front of her. She wondered again why he always seemed so familiar to her. She never met him before she came to work here.

"Are you in a hurry? Want some experience tonight?"

Erin instinctively backed up. "Experience in what?"

"Relax, nothing bad. I need to get some kids out of the drunk tank. Wanna go? Could be a chance of a lifetime. Nothing like drunk college kids. But you wouldn't know, would you?"

"I don't have much time for partying." Erin saw the book on her desk.

"Just as well. It is overrated. Want to accompany

me? The car is outside."

Erin learned little in the quick drive to the jail. Several college kids were arrested for DUI and Public Drunk at a party and were being released into their parents' custody.

Sitting on a bench in the front of the jail office, Erin watched Cronkite talk to the night clerk. Evidently, she could not go inside with him. There were several irritated parents on the other side of the room clustered together but not talking. One of the parents must have known Cronkite and called him to do the dirty work. Several of them eyed her.

Erin fidgeted on the wooden bench feeling guilty for something—even though she did not know what. Maybe just being in this atmosphere made her feel that way. She could hear the booming voice of Cronkite in the room next door. It sounded friendly at first and then angry. Someone was being read the riot act.

Eventually the door opened, and several girls stumbled out; all garbed in party dresses with smeared makeup, one missing a shoe. They were met in the middle of the room by their parents. Some were hugged, others shoved roughly toward the door. And then she saw her. Sally Elkman came out last just in front of Cronkite. Her tear stained face searched the room for her ride. She stopped when she saw Erin— then quickly turned her head.

"Where's your mother, young lady?" Cronkite closed the door behind him.

"I don't know. I called her."

"Well, I'm not waiting all night. You can just go back in there for all I care."

Erin realized she stared and glanced away.

"I really need a bathroom." Sally pleaded with Cronkite.

"Not one in your cell?"

"I mean a real bathroom." The haughty glare returned. Sally could not be expected to use a toilet surrounded by others.

Cronkite sighed. "Erin, can you escort this young lady to the bathroom. And Sally, you'd better not cause any trouble or I'm coming in after you myself." He nodded to Erin. "Down the hall and to the left."

Erin stood. She glanced first at Sally and then at Cronkite. He nodded. Instinctively she reached for Sally's arm, who pulled away. "This way," she said leading her down the hall.

"So, got a job at the jail these days?" Sally smelled like day-old-booze as she wobbled by and opened the door to the metal stall. Erin gagged as she heard retching and turned on the water to keep from losing her own dinner.

Sally emerged moments later and drank from the sink scooping water with her hand.

"I work for Cronkite." Erin replied to the question posed moments before.

"Hah! Work? Doing what?"

Nothing had changed since high school. Sally wanted to be in charge. "Evidently taking drunks to the bathroom. You ready?" Erin gestured toward the door and Sally stumbled out. Her short red dress wrinkled and puckered up from sitting. A flash of panty showed as she wobbled down the hall on three-inch heels to match the dress. Erin shook her head.

Out front a woman talking with Cronkite suddenly rushed to embrace Sally. "Okay Mom. Can we just go?" Sally pulled away from the woman—an older version of herself. Sally's mother nodded at Cronkite and she and her daughter left together.

"You know those kids?" Cronkite asked when they got back to the car.

"Only Sally Elkman. We went to school together."

"Cute little Sally Elkman has sure changed in the last few years. I've known the family for a long time. She used to sit on my lap when I had dinner at their house. Before her dad left and she and her mother struggled to make ends meet."

"I didn't know about her dad. We aren't friends or anything."

He pulled his car up next to hers in the parking lot. "So, you got your first experience bailing out a drunk. How was it?"

"Interesting." Erin climbed out of the car and pulled her keys from her pocket.

"See you in the morning," he said as he drove away.

"In the morning." Erin suddenly realized the book still sat in her office. "Damn, I'll never get any studying done!" She walked again to the locked and gloomy back door pulling her keys from her pocket.

Inside, the darkness and quiet once again overwhelmed her. The always-present emergency lights were on in the cavernous dark hallways. She crept down the hall toward her cubicle as quietly as she could and wondered why she felt the need not to disturb the silent office. She rounded the corner to her cubicle, and there lay the book on the corner of the desk; right where she intended to pick it up last time. The text lay next to the law book Cronkite had in his hand when they left.

113

She would place it in his office for him if he left it unlocked. Sometimes he forgot to lock it. Walking to the door, which stood ajar, she fumbled for the light switch.

"Oh yes!" a woman's deep throaty voice echoed from the office of one of the most prestigious attorneys in Tulsa. But she just left him in the parking lot and saw him drive away.

Erin started to walk away, but she knocked over the plant that always sat on the table next to the door and instinctively flipped the light switch.

The woman's head hung over the edge of the desk with her long dark hair draped over the side. The figure on top of her lifted his head and gazed straight into Erin's eyes. Nathan! But why Cronkite's office? Her first impulse said run away. Oh, God, why did she turn on the light?

"What are you doing in here?" Erin demanded in a tone that belied her age and authority.

"I could ask you the same question," came the reply as he stood pulling up his pants. Only then did the woman glance back at Erin attempting to cover herself with her arms. Stephanie, the receptionist, who had been rude to her since the day she walked in the door for who knew what reason. Nathan and Stephanie? On Cronkite's desk?

Erin stood grounded. She wanted to run. She wanted to yell at him. Had he no shame? On the boss's desk? But mostly she wished she had never turned on the light. "Putting up a book." She turned to leave.

"Wait, Erin. I want to talk to you." She could hear Nathan coming after her.

Erin walked away as fast as she could, headed for

the back door of the office, trying to get the image out of her mind of her naked co-workers on the desk of a man she had come to respect and care about. Like the father she didn't have anymore. And then it hit her why he always seemed so familiar to her. The aftershave he wore, the same as Dad's. A scent she associated with him. No wonder Cronkite seemed like a father figure to her.

Nathan quickly caught up to her and grabbed her arm, his shirt thrown on and unbuttoned. He stood before her with hair ruffled and tell-tale lipstick on his neck. Erin knew his neck was not the only place the lipstick had stained.

"What do you want?" She pulled her arm from his grasp and tried not to allow her voice to quaver as she spoke.

"I just want to talk to you." He had never spoken to her so kindly. He smiled.

"I don't want to talk to you."

"Erin, listen. I know you are just a young girl and what you saw may have frightened you, but really Stephanie and I are dating."

"Yeah, dating." She tried to walk away but he stepped in front of her.

"Don't go. We aren't finished." He smiled a wicked smile. "I just need to know how you feel about this. We didn't mean to scare you. We were just— expressing our feelings for each other."

Erin's face warmed as she seethed. She didn't appreciate being treated like a child. "Is that what you call it? Fucking the receptionist on the boss's desk is expressing your feelings? Your feelings for her, or about him?"

"Don't get excited. It's nothing. Just go home and we'll forget the whole thing ever happened." He turned to walk away.

"I'm not forgetting anything." She instantly regretted her words.

He turned back to her slowly. The smile now replaced with a smirk. "You listen to me little girl. You don't want to go there. I'll bury you before you ever get started." He walked closer to her his face darkening as he approached. "You didn't see anything tonight and tomorrow when you come in you will report directly to my desk. You're mine now." She could smell the whiskey on his breath. His nose almost touched hers.

She paused, deeply staring into his intense eyes. He had threatened before—not his first time, nor would it be his last. He had her right where he wanted. The next move hers. She took a deep breath thinking of the first time he ran her from the conference room. She knew he could end a career that hadn't even begun.

"Or what?" she said more calmly than she felt.

They stared at each other for what seemed like an eternity when Stephanie emerged from the office fully dressed and pushed past Erin as she walked down the hall.

"You're wrong." Erin's hands became fists. "I don't belong to anyone." She walked away with her school book in her hand, down the hall toward the back door and freedom.

"Okay, what do you want?" Nathan called to her as she walked away. She didn't respond but kept walking until she got to her car. She pulled away from the parking lot and saw him in her rearview mirror and then turned the corner. Then she began to shake, and the tears spilled down her cheeks.

Chapter 16

Erin stared at search engines all morning. Blinking, her eye lids felt like sand paper on dried-out orbs. Finding nothing in People Search, she moved to others. She found the woman had moved back into the state. In fact, in the county within reach of the boy's father. She checked and re-checked. Yes, all the search engines had the same address. Would the DMV confirm an address? And if not, would a utility company? Everyone needed utilities. She picked up the phone and dialed her aunt's extension as she saved her latest information onto the flash drive and dropped it in her pocket.

"Cronkite and Associates," crooned the receptionist who turned her back on Erin most days as she entered the building.

"Um, Stephanie, this is Erin. Is Aunt Toni in?" Erin knew she shouldn't have used the word aunt.

"Ms. Stone is in court this afternoon." Stephanie sighed with resignation like Erin should instinctively know this fact. These days Stephanie treated her even more poorly than she had before the night Erin caught her and Nathan in Cronkite's office.

"Okay, thanks." Erin hung up. No sense in arguing with her. No one would ever win.

Checking the internet Yellow Pages, she found the number of the DMV and dialed. She waited on the line forever going through menu after menu and talking to robots on the other end. Irritated she finally hung up and tried the electric company. Most people had electricity even if they didn't have gas. She would start there. Karen Little would not use her real name for a utility company. Samantha Smith—the last name she used might be right. Erin dialed the customer service number.

"This is Erin Sampson, I work for Cronkite and Associates. We have an ongoing case and I wondered if you could give me some information about a customer of yours named Samantha Smith? I want to check an address I have and see if she is still living at that address."

The woman on the other end took a moment and checked her records. Erin could hear her typing into the database that held all the secrets of its many members.

"I have a Samantha Smith at 22319 West Highway 51. Is that the one you want?"

"Is that a 911 address?"

"Yes, ma'am we use the current addresses that have been assigned to the rural areas for emergency services."

"And she is still residing there?" Erin could not believe her good luck. Could she still live at that address?

"I show she paid her last bill ten days ago and there are no outstanding charges."

"So, she is still there?" Erin twisted around in her chair and wrote on the legal pad.

"It appears so. I mean why would she pay her bill if not? I show no late payments, so she is not catching up anything."

"Could you give me your name in case I need to

call you again?" Erin suddenly felt giddy with excitement.

"My name is Inez Manner and I am a Customer Service Representative for the Coop."

"Inez, you've made my day. Thank you so much for your help." Erin tossed the pen in the air in celebration.

"Thank you. Is there anything else that you need at this time?"

"No, that is all. Thank you again." Erin hung up the phone still unable to believe she had done it.

She had her! She found Karen Little and hopefully the boy too. She picked up her notes and ran to Cronkite's office. He would want to know right away. Rounding the corner, she ran smack into Nathan with his head down reading as he walked.

"Sorry," she mumbled as she tried to get past him. He stepped in her way. She scanned his face and remembered the way he looked the night in the boss's office as he stood and pulled up his pants.

"Where are you going in such a hurry?"

"Sorry, I need to see Mr. Cronkite." Erin tried to sidestep him.

"Well, that's a problem. He's out this afternoon." His face showed the smirk Erin had come to know.

Deflated, Erin realized the two people she trusted the most in the firm were not in and she had news. She knew better than to tell anyone else. But someone needed to know about the discovery. She could send Cronkite an email and maybe he would check his phone.

"Well, I'll talk to him later, then." She backed away and turned to walk back down the hall to her laptop that held all the critical information she found about the case. She needed to keep this under wraps until she could alert Cronkite.

"Erin, can I see you a moment?" Sara stood outside her office gesturing for her to come in.

"Of course." Erin walked in still giddy with the anticipation of talking to Cronkite. She had cracked the case!

"I wanted to let you know that Mr. Cronkite has approved a raise for you beginning on the next pay period. I know we were a little slow since it has been more than ninety days, but he's impressed with your work and wanted to let you know."

"Well, that's great! I'd tell him thanks if he were here." The day just kept getting better.

"Oh, he's here somewhere."

"Nathan said he took the afternoon off."

"Not to my knowledge. I think he is just taking a long lunch."

"Great. Thank you, Sara, and if you see him, would you let him know I have something to talk to him about?" She could hardly contain the joy and needed to share with someone.

"Of course. Things going well on the case he put you on?"

"Yes, I think so." Erin felt badly not confiding in Sara, but she could only discuss the case with Cronkite. "Thanks again." Erin nodded, smiled, and walked back down the hall.

Opening the door of the board room, she suddenly realized people were in the room. She had only been gone a moment, but all her documents were stacked on a side table. Erin had no idea whose clients these belonged to, but she needed to get to her laptop. She walked in and began rummaging through the pile of files—the laptop nowhere. She hadn't been gone five minutes.

"Okay, we can get started." Nathan stepped in with a bottle of water in his hand and looked directly at her.

"Excuse me, but did you see the laptop here just a minute ago?" Erin examined the face of the man she felt nothing but hate for.

"We have a meeting. You'll have to search later."

"But it was here not five minutes ago." She stared at the files stacked in a pile on the floor. No computer.

"Come back later, we need this room."

He did this because he thought Cronkite left and could get away with it. Erin stood with the note in her hand that held scribbled information from the woman at the electric coop. In her pocket she felt the flash drive with all the information she had obtained. If it came down to it, she could put the flash drive in her own computer at home. But what had happened to the laptop? She walked out the door and down the hall.

**\*\*\*\***

"Don't say anything to anybody." Cronkite had been emphatic in his response when she called his cell phone to tell him about the laptop. "I know what goes on in my law firm and I will take care of it."

Erin didn't know what to say. Did he think she had lost it? He had to realize she would never do such a thing. His voice sounded angry—at someone. Maybe at her.

"I didn't talk to anyone but you, and like I said I have a copy of everything. I think I have what is needed to find the mother and I can prove it. I talked to the electric cooperative and they think she is still there. I charted out everything like you told me and I saved it—twice. I never thought about anyone stealing my work."

"It is not your fault, Erin. We'll find it. And if we don't you still have the evidence we need. You are a smart girl. I don't blame you for anything. We'll get with I.T. and check out a new computer. And I'll get to the bottom of this, I guarantee it."

Chapter 17

The car bounced over broken concrete in the driveway of Erin's house just as her mother walked out the door, keys in hand. They hardly saw each other anymore. Pulling to her side of the driveway, she waved.

"You leaving?" Erin opened the car door that no longer squeaked.

"Going to clean the shop. How was your day?"

"Busy." Erin knew she couldn't talk to Mom about the stolen laptop or anything else that had happened at the firm recently. Mom would instantly tell Aunt Toni. She needed to be taken seriously and having your mother and aunt fight your battles would not work. "Want some help?"

"Oh, honey, you just finished working. Go relax."

"No, really, let me change and I'll join you. You know it goes faster with two."

Erin cleaned the buckets with hot soapy water while her mother wiped down the shelves of the cooler. A clean shop made the flowers last longer her mom always said. But Erin knew the drill. After taking out the trash they would sweep and mop the floors and then be done.

"Want to put some chicken on the grill after we get finished?" Alice stuck her head out of the cooler and held the door open with a gloved hand.

"Sure, that sounds good. The grill hasn't had much use lately."

"Well, if we were ever home at the same time…"

"I know. I hate that. But I love my classes."

"And the job?" Alice wiped the glass shelf dry.

"Yeah, and the job."

"Sometimes it is hard to tell. You're so tired all the time I can't tell if you like it or not."

"It is just different, that's all. Not like when you work for your mother all the time. Oh, and I got a raise today. I don't know how much, but at least they like me." Erin stacked the bucket on top of the others under the sink.

"That's great! How could they not? Anyway, your aunt is there if you need something and you know you can always go to her."

"I know." Erin dried the last bucket and wiped up the water around the industrial sized sink.

"I hope they aren't working you too hard and your studies suffer. I worry about how much time you spend on the road late at night."

"I'm fine." Erin grabbed the trash sack and tied it shut, carrying it to the back as her mother instinctively picked up the broom. They danced well-choreographed movements performed many times.

The lights blinked in the store—a message to begin closing the departments and rushing out the last of the shoppers, assisting them with their purchases.

"You know," Alice said around a bite of chicken once they were home, "you could think about moving to Tulsa and not driving so far every day. We could afford the room and board for the dorms."

"And leave you by yourself?"

"I'm not by myself. I have friends and co-workers. And there is always your Aunt Toni."

"Except that Aunt Toni is in Tulsa too." Erin wiped her mouth with the paper napkin that sat in the holder on the table.

"It wouldn't be that far away."

"I know. It just doesn't seem right, somehow. Leaving you, I mean. Dad left—not on purpose of course, but he left—and now me? I mean that's not fair."

"Sweetheart, are you still mad at your dad for leaving us?"

"No, I never felt mad at him, just sad. Anyway, I don't want to leave you alone."

"Well, I'm not alone. Like I said, I have friends."

The phone rang in midsentence and Erin glanced at the caller ID. "Brent Taylor" it said.

"Your friend," Erin said with a smile. She knew her mom had been seeing a lot of him lately.

"Hi Brent. No, Erin and I are eating chicken we barbequed. We finally got around to using the grill before cold weather."

"Ask him over," Erin whispered to her mom who waved her off. "Do it. It's okay."

"Want to join us?" Alice blushed lightly when she spoke. "Erin is here, and it was her idea."

Erin rolled her eyes. Great. She would end up chaperoning the adults.

"Okay, maybe next time. We'll plan something in advance. Okay, talk to you later." Alice hung up the phone.

"Is he coming over?" Erin took her plate to the sink.

"No, he had things to do."

"Or he didn't want to put up with the kid."

"Oh Erin. He likes you. He has kids of his own, you know."

"No, I didn't know. How old are they?"

"A boy and a girl both younger than you. Still in high school."

"Have you met them?"

"No not yet. We've been talking about how to get all of us together and maybe do something."

"Cool." Erin cleared the dishes and wondered what it would be like to have brothers and sisters as Mom loaded the dishwasher.

That night Erin slept fitfully. She dreamed about lost laptops, hidden children, and moving day, all jumbled together as she tossed and turned.

Chapter 18

Jake Hardridge walked across the TU campus in the crisp autumn air. Sweatshirt weather, his mother called it. She loved this weather and probably wore a sweatshirt at home today. Leaves swirled around his feet, some still not crisp, but they were falling just the same. Jake a sophomore this year—still undecided on a major—tinkered with the idea of accounting. No, maybe law like his old man. More than likely it would be business, a generic enough major to get him through his college years, with no idea what he wanted to do. It seemed only yesterday he played tennis at his dad's country club. He loved tennis and computers, but unsure what, if anything, to do with them in life.

He smiled at the undergrads creating an impromptu Frisbee game on campus. These kids never seemed to go to class. Hard to blame them on a day like today though. Monarchs were floating by on their travels to Mexico. Cold weather on the way. Maybe he'd like to follow the Monarchs. He wanted to travel, but his dad wasn't going to fund a vagabond. He had to earn that one himself.

"Hi Jake!" A gaggle of sorority girls called to him as they walked by. He knew them from parties at the frat house. Cute girls, but not his type. Like his major, still unsure of what his type was, he knew it was a girl with something on her mind besides parties and clothes.

He normally tried to get out of the frat house prior to the weekend parties and seek the quiet of the library, but sometimes he got stuck. He began locking his door—never much of a party animal—and soon found he could shimmy down the drain pipe just outside his window if necessary. He had no idea how long the pipe would last under his weight.

But girls were still a mystery to him. They were one of the reasons he didn't get involved in the parties. Not only were the parties noisy—how could you meet and talk to someone at those things—but they were just not his style. He talked to a cute girl named Julie once, and when the house became so noisy you couldn't hear yourself think, he asked her if she would like to go somewhere else to talk. Thinking he had something else in mind, she stormed away and hadn't talked to him since, even though he wished she would.

Finally, he gave in and took a date to a frat party. Not really a date, his dad's bailiff. She didn't get out much being a single mother. Thinking she might like to mingle with people her own age he asked her along. It wasn't long before she disappeared at the frat house.

"Has anyone seen Nicole? You know the girl I came in with in the white skirt?" Jake stood in the kitchen of the frat house. Somehow most of the student body showed up uninvited at the party that night. A girl in a shiny blue top gestured with her thumb toward the living room.

In the living room he glanced around. Circling the room once more with his eyes he saw Newman leaning in with his hand on the mantel of the fireplace. Someone stood between him and the fireplace. He recognized the white skirt and shapely legs as Nicole's.

Why were women drawn to Newman like moths to a flame? She ended up spending the evening with Newman and Jake tried not to be jealous. They came as friends not really dating, he told himself. Later he heard she went out with Todd Newman. Not for long. Most girls didn't date him for very long. He loved to brag about his conquests and they probably found out.

Nicole's sweet personality endeared her to everyone. She had a baby while still in high school and would probably be a college student now if not for the child. Currently she lived with her grandmother and baby boy while she worked. She talked about going back to school someday but for now, she needed to work. The relationship with Todd didn't last long. Jake wondered if she knew Todd's real personality. It was not for him to judge. Maybe he'd ask her out again now that he knew she didn't date Newman anymore. Maybe a real date this time.

The wind came up and he pulled the hood up on his sweatshirt covering his bright red hair. His ears warmed making him feel warm all over.

Cool temps and bright sun made for a perfect autumn day. He had a computer lab coming up and he needed to be on time. No time for games with the students on campus who never went to class, and no time for sorority girls or parties. He needed to get going.

Inside the cold and dry computer lab—exactly the way a computer liked it—Jake was glad for the sweatshirt. The lab four hours long, Jake knew the warmth of the sweatshirt would not be enough before it was done.

## Chapter 19

Todd sat in the bar waiting on his brother. Outside the wind howled in a winter storm likely to get bad this time. The first storm of the season—and before Christmas. Todd, underage, took out his genuine-looking ID. The bartender didn't seem concerned about serving him. He waited on is brother, Paul. And likely Paul would have friends with him. Paul might be the only person he really respected. His professors were like Dad, only interested in his grades. And his friends these days—if he had any—were just a bunch of assholes interested in his money. The one thing the Newmans had plenty of. Most of the campus knew it. Dad contributed each year to the alumni association. That assured his sons getting into college and the fraternity he'd belonged to. Todd and Paul were chips off the old block. Not true, but Dad liked to think it so. And what Dad wanted, Dad got.

Todd swirled the beer in the bottom of the glass, drained it and signaled the bartender. Paul was late. Over in the corner sat a nice-looking girl in a short skirt who just might help him pass the time. He could show her the Alpha Romeo outside and offer her a ride. That one worked with most girls. Some of them wanted to drive it but most were attracted to its sleek lines. Sleek, like he found theirs.

He stood to walk her way just as the door banged

open and in walked Paul with several brothers from the house. Todd waved. He had carefully chosen a booth in the corner—away from the rest of the noise—so he and his brother could talk. The rest of the crowd would end up at the pool table anyway. Todd sighed as the girl got up to go to the bathroom, so he turned to his brother.

"Hey, bro, you're late."

"Sorry. It's not my fault. These old ladies couldn't decide which dress to wear."

Todd laughed as they all settled into the booth. The waitress walked over with menus.

"Whatcha drinkin'?" She popped her bubble gum and glanced up at the TV, obviously bored.

They all ordered beers on tap and then studied the menu to decide between burgers and nachos—the standard fare of college kids. After ordering, Paul's friends wandered over to the pool table leaving them alone.

"So, how's college life in the dorms?" Paul poked at him. Todd could not live in the fraternity house until next year.

"Oh man. Those toads never shut up and let you get any studying done. It is just party, party, party. And not the good kind—just TVs blaring and loud music. I have to go to the library to study."

"Well, at least you're studying. Good to hear." Paul sipped his beer. "How's Mom and Dad?"

"I don't see them any more than I have to." Both boys glanced away. Todd was sure his brother had the same type thoughts—best just to stay away.

"Mom is getting worse. Well, so is Dad. But Mom just seems to be crawling into her own little world. She gets out of bed about noon and spends the afternoon with her cronies at the club. And Dad—well, Dad is Dad." Todd swigged a large amount of liquid, stared at the glass, and sat it down next to the wet ring on the table. The pretty girl walked back to her table and Todd's eyes followed her every movement. Cute, but his main attention needed to be directed at his brother tonight.

"Well, you're out now. I don't mind telling you that there were times I never thought I would get out." Paul took a swig of beer.

Todd nodded then glanced at the girl again.

"Hey, man, am I boring you?"

"No, of course not."

"Cute though, huh? She has a boyfriend. One of the guys in the house. Can't remember her name."

"Well, maybe she DID have a boyfriend at the house. But maybe she'd like a change." Todd smiled around the glass.

"You and women. I don't get it. You love 'em and then you leave 'em. When are you going to find a nice girl, and settle down?"

"You sound like Mom and Dad. Besides, maybe I don't like nice girls." Todd smiled at his brother over the top of his glass.

"Well you play around now because someday you won't be able to."

"I'm never gettin' married, man. That stuff just brings you down."

"Yeah, we'll see. The bigger they are the harder they fall." Paul stood and walked toward the pool table with his friends. Todd watched for a minute—then decided if his brother wasn't going to stay and talk, he might as well leave.

When the food arrived, Todd could not be found, and neither could the cute girl in the short skirt.

Much too early the next morning, someone banged on the door of Todd's dorm room calling his name. They could wait. He needed to sleep. He drank too much last night and still needed a few more hours to sleep it off. He dozed back off and the noise started again. Then a key shoved in the keyhole and someone opened the door.

"Todd Newman?" a voice of authority called out from the door. The campus police along with some other uniforms stood in his room and he viewed them through a hung-over haze.

"Get dressed. You're coming with us."

Chapter 20

Erin had to admit getting to class and work saved time since she moved into the dorms on campus. Luckily, she picked up a room someone had given up when they dropped out after first semester. Erin moved into the room just down the hall from Bernadette after Christmas. Erin hoped she and Bernadette could room together, but Bernadette's roommate had other ideas. Getting into the dorm in the middle of the year could be tricky sometimes.

Alice helped Erin move into the dorm and they both cried. Erin called her mother every night.

Studying remained a problem. Her roommate had the TV on when she was home. And if she wasn't home, there was always noise down the hall. Erin wondered how students got any studying done.

But some people didn't go to college to study. And it seemed some people didn't need to study, they just absorbed it all in class. Like Rob, a sponge, who put in more hours working in the library than were probably legal under the rules but was always at the top of his class. He often said he wasted his money on a room since he lived at the library.

"Are you meeting Rob at the library again?" Bernadette sat curled up with books in her normal position on the bed. Erin didn't think Bernadette could study without clutter.

"Yes, he isn't working this evening."

"He almost lives there. If he isn't working there, he is studying at the library. I think he has a table with his name on it."

"You need anything while I'm out?" Erin in her socks pulled on the snow boots she had purchased that weekend just before the first snow of the season.

"I don't think so. Let me know when you get in."

"You sound like my mother."

"A girl can't be too careful, and it gets dark early this time of year."

"See you later, Mom." Erin giggled as she threw the scarf around her neck and closed the door.

Tromping through the snow toward the library she kept to the lighted area. Sparkling snow swirled under the lamps like crystals. She found the evening cool but not as cold as she thought and unwound her scarf breathing deeply the night air. She could see the library in the distance. She plotted a path under the twinkling lights. The shuttle came past going the other way. It made a circle around the inner campus and she used it often, but not tonight. Erin couldn't remember the last time she put gas in her car.

She never saw him coming as he rounded the corner until he ran smack into her as she stared up into the starry night.

"Sorry," she mumbled under her breath.

She remembered Bernadette telling her to be careful. Another student on campus was to be expected. But not this student. The boy with his hands shoved deep into the pockets of his Pea Coat and a stocking cap pulled low on his head did not expect her either. He stopped and turned around and stared directly into her eyes. Todd. Her breath caught in her chest.

A crooked smile crossed his lips.

"Erin, isn't it?"

"Todd."

"I haven't seen you on campus. Whatcha been doin' girl?" He stepped forward.

She turned to walk away.

"Wait, I'm just saying hi." He came around from behind and faced her.

"You said it." She turned slightly to move around him.

"Well, be rude why don't you! I'm just being friendly." He walked backward in front of her as she tried to get around him. "You know you don't have to be like that."

"Go away."

"Whoa! Just like that, huh? I thought we had something."

Erin stopped in her tracks. It wasn't what he said but how he said it. She felt threatened. Again. First the prom and now this. After the incident with Nathan at work, it seemed threats were getting to be a habit and she didn't like it.

She walked closer to the boy she once thought she wanted to date. "Go away, Todd. I don't want to talk to you. We had nothing. We never did. Now leave me alone."

He stared at her, unblinking.

"Erin!" a shout came from near the library and she saw Rob trotting her way.

"Coming!" she called back and shoved past the boy who had humiliated her at the prom walking away quickly. The senior prom seemed like a million years ago.

When she met Rob, she grabbed his arm and kissed him on the cheek, turning him toward the library.

"Cold," she said and walked him away.

"Who was that?" Rob walked arm in arm with her glancing behind him.

"Just a student I ran into. Do you have a table?"

"Always." They walked up the steps to the welcome warmth of the library.

\*\*\*\*

Erin stretched loudly and pushed the chair away from the desk. Students glanced up from their books and the librarian stared in a way meant to hush her. She had been sitting too long.

"Bathroom break." She patted Rob on the shoulder walking away. Near the bathroom she saw the rail-thin boy with red hair. She knew him but could not place a name with the face. He nodded. Erin nodded back and opened the door to the women's restroom. Inside the familiar smell of a public bathroom. Students came and went from the stalls, some washing their hands others spreading what germs they picked up along the way. She stepped into the first open stall she found.

"Anyway, I heard he was arrested for rape. With his money, his old man will probably get him off though." A voice could be heard over the flush of toilets and running water.

"Really? I can't believe that."

"I can." A response from the same area of the bathroom picked up the thread of conversation.

"What do you mean? Todd Newman, rape? Why would he when he can have any girl he wants."

Erin's ears picked up at the familiar name.

138

"Have you ever gone out with him?"

"No, have you?"

"Yes, and it wasn't pleasant. I won't ever do it again. I can believe it. Let's just say he insisted."

Erin walked out of the stall to the sink, stunned. Could the conversation be true? Todd arrested? If so, he made bail. She watched the girls gathered around the trash can and knew she had seen them on campus before.

The outside door to the bathroom slammed shut as the girls left and Erin finished washing her hands.

Back in the hall the red-headed boy stood waiting for her. But still she could not put a name to his face.

"Erin?"

"Yes," she said hoping she would not have to come up with a name. "I'm Jake Hardridge. I met you at my dad's office the other day. You are a friend of Nicole's?"

That's where she knew him. "Well, yes. I know her."

"I just wondered if you knew—is she mad at me or something? I hate to ask, but has she mentioned me?"

"I really don't talk to her that often." The conversation surprised Erin. Had Nicole said they were good friends? She really didn't know the girl that well.

"Well, we went out once—sort of—not really a date, but I asked her out the other day and she said no. I don't know, maybe she had a sick baby or something."

"She has a baby?"

"Yes, you didn't know? "

"Like I said, we really don't talk that often. Just work stuff." Erin fidgeted, the strange conversation making her uncomfortable.

"Oh, I'm sorry, I thought you two were friends. Anyway, I really like her and wanted to take her out. She has been acting kinda weird lately."

"I don't really know her that well. But some guy tried to force himself on her lately. That is what we were talking about the day you walked in. I hope that wasn't a secret because she didn't say I could talk about it." Erin glanced at the table where she and Rob sat. He was not there.

"I didn't know anything about it. Who did she go out with?"

"She didn't say." Erin smiled as Rob walked up with his books under one arm and hers under the other.

"I'm about beat. You?" He handed her the books.

"Yes, me too. Rob this is Jake Hardridge. His father is a judge and we met the other day at the courthouse."

Rob stuck out his hand. "Rob Anderson," he said. "Nice to meet you."

"And you." The two shook hands eyeing Erin.

"I'm sorry Jake, I don't know much about Nicole, but good luck. I need to get back to the dorm."

Rob and Erin walked away as Rob asked, "You met the judge's son?"

"Yes. The judge's bailiff is named Nicole. She told me the other day about some guy she went out with that tried to rape her."

"That guy?" Rob's face turned dark.

"No, someone else. She told me the story when Jake walked in. Obviously, Nicole didn't want him to see her crying. Anyway, I guess Jake has a crush on Nicole and he asked me why she wouldn't go out with him. I really don't know, but maybe she is running scared after the last time. However, I just found out she is a mother too. So, she has a double reason to be careful of men."

"Sad. Some guys are really stupid."

"Not like you." Erin smiled at the boy who opened the door for her as she wound the scarf around her neck again.

"No, not like me. Speaking of which, to prove that I'm not stupid, I want to officially ask you out on a real honest-to-God, date. You know the kind where we get dressed up and I take you to a nice restaurant and maybe a movie? Not just meet at the library?"

Erin stopped and stared at the boy in front of her.

"Now don't get all edgy again." Rob threaded his arm through the crook in her elbow. "It is not an invitation to spend the rest of your life with me. Just a date. I think we deserve it. Besides, I want to show you a good time and point out that I know how to treat a lady."

"A date." Erin fingered the scarf around her neck.

"A real-life date."

"Like when?"

"How's Saturday night?" He raised one eyebrow in question.

"I go home most weekends."

"Me too. We live in the same town, remember?"

Erin glanced out at the darkened campus and then back at the boy who sacked groceries in the store they both worked in when they were in high school. She liked his company and if he wanted to show her a good time, she could deal with that.

"Okay. What time?"

Rob smiled the broadest smile she had ever seen

cross his geek-type engineering face. He might have just won a marathon by the expression on his face.

"How's 7:00 sound?"

"Sounds great." She smiled.

Arm in arm they walked across the dark camps toward the dorms. The trip back warmer than the trip out. Maybe dating wasn't such a bad idea after all.

Chapter 21

"Mom, which of these shoes go with this dress?" Erin stood barefoot in the living room with a pair of heels and a pair of ballet flats in her hands.

"I think it is snowing again." Her mother glanced up from the paper.

"Ugh! I'm so sick of winter." The doorbell rang. "He's not supposed to be here yet!" She turned and ran back toward her bedroom.

"I'll get it. Maybe some boots with a skirt?"

Alice walked to the door and opened it to find petite Bernadette stomping her feet to rid herself of the snow that crusted them.

"Hi, Bernadette, come in. Erin is in her room going crazy over what to wear. Maybe you can restore her sanity." Alice ushered her in and then went back to the newspaper.

Bernadette knocked on the door to Erin's room not waiting for an answer before walking in.

"Help me!" Erin stood in the middle of the room in a sleeveless dress with shoes all over the floor.

"Okay, first you have the wrong season. That is a cute summer dress. It is snowing outside, and you need boots."

"That's what Mom said."

"Well, she's right. Let's start with the closet." Bernadette rummaged through the overstuffed closet that Erin seldom used. She had another one at school full of jeans for class and things she wore to work. "Oh, this is cute. I've never seen you wear this sweater dress."

"My aunt gave it to me. It is too low cut to wear."

"Scarf? Could you tie a scarf, so the neckline doesn't show? Do you have tights to go with it?"

"I don't know. I have cream, and brown and some others I can't find. They might be at school." Erin threw tights from the open drawer digging even deeper to find others.

"Your boots are brown, right? How about some brown tights with the burgundy dress? That will work."

"I don't know if I have any scarves that are the right color."

Alice stuck her head in the door. "Looks like a tornado hit this room. You girls finding something?"

"Mom, do you have a scarf that will go with this dress?" Erin held up the sweater dress from her aunt's closet.

"I might. Let me see." Alice walked down the hall toward her bedroom.

"I can't believe I am going to this much trouble for Rob. I mean this is silly. I've known him for years and now I'm panicking."

"It's a girl thing. We just want to be perfect, that is all." Bernadette hung the clothes back up that were thrown on the bed. "He's a great guy though. I'm so glad you finally came to your senses."

"Came to my senses? You mean I'm not stupid anymore?" Dressed in the tights and sweater dress, Erin rummaged for earrings.

"You were never stupid, just scared, I think."

"Yeah, I guess scared is the right word. I don't want to get distracted and not finish school, you know?"

"You're too smart for that." Bernadette crossed the room, her arms loaded with hangers holding clothing. She could barely see over the top of them. "You know we are going to organize this mess one of these days. I mean really, you have some cute stuff, but you have no idea where it is. You could be wearing some of it to work and class."

"I know. In my spare time." Erin hooked the ruby colored earrings in her ear lobes.

"Well, tonight you go out with the cute boy. Next time it is you and me, sister, we'll order a pizza and organize this mess."

"You've got it."

The doorbell rang as Alice brought in an armload of scarves. "I'll get it," she said dumping the scarves on the bed.

**** 

Erin sat across the table from Rob in the darkened corner of the restaurant. The candle flickered on the table as the waiter brought fresh bread and handed them menus.

"Rob, this is terribly expensive. Are you sure?" Erin scanned down the list of entrees.

"I'm sure. I can take a girl out for a nice dinner— now and then."

"I know but really we could have ordered a pizza." Pizza could not be found on this menu.

"No, it is a date. Now relax. We are going to have a nice romantic dinner just like in the movies."

"Like in the movies, huh?"

"Or something like that." Rob unrolled the silverware in the napkin and laid it beside the plate.

"You know I don't have to have this, right? I'm happy just to be with you."

Rob smiled broadly. "Yes, that is what makes it even more special. You're the type of girl who doesn't need to be wined and dined."

"The wine list, sir." The waiter dutifully handed Rob the long menu with a list of wines.

"No, we won't be having wine." He handed the menu back.

The waiter nodded and walked away. Erin's hand to her mouth, she giggled. "Do you really think he would have served us?"

"I don't know. Maybe we appear old enough."

"Well, I've got to say, you showed up dressed nicely tonight. You're very handsome."

"You look great too. I've never seen that dress." Erin glanced down and readjusted the scarf.

"My aunt. I may never need to go shopping again." She unfolded the napkin and laid it in her lap.

"She asked for Perrier! What she wants is Perrier!" a familiar voice from across the room roared. All heads turned his way.

Both Rob and Erin jerked around to see where the voice came from. Todd. He accompanied a girl in a tight dress who appeared stricken. Eyes downcast she was embarrassed over the outburst.

"Well, so much for a quiet evening." Rob's eyes narrowed. He took a drink of water and looked at Erin. "I'm sure he's too busy to notice us."

"Perfect. Of all the people to bump into." She breathed deeply. "He is not going to ruin this evening, though. Who knows, maybe he'll leave."

But of course, he didn't. Just as heaping plates of spaghetti arrived for Rob and Erin, Todd began anew. He banged his fork on the glass to get the attention of the overworked waiter.

"We're out of bread," he hissed loudly. Erin knew Todd marveled at making people uncomfortable. But tonight, she would not be taken down by him. Could he be drunk? At least he hadn't seen them.

Erin swirled the spaghetti onto the fork and smiled at her date. She thought of the cartoon with two dogs and a plate of pasta. She and Rob both ordered the same thing. She knew he was confused over the menu, but aside from the salad dressing the orders were identical. The bread could have made a meal. The aroma of the yeast bread welcomed them to the Italian kitchen when they came in from the snow. Warm atmosphere, glowing candles, and Italian music played softly in the background, she wondered if Rob had scouted this place out before he came.

"Dessert sir?" The waiter appeared instantly at Rob's elbow with a dessert tray as soon as he put down his fork.

Rob raised his head to see Erin as she groaned. "Want to share something?" His eyes pleaded for dessert.

"I'll have to join a gym if this keeps up."

"We'll make it small."

"Okay, you choose." Erin wiped her mouth and replaced the napkin.

"Waiter!" Todd yelled from the other side of the restaurant. The girl gone. Had she left him or maybe just gone to the bathroom?

Rob pointed to the dessert of choice and told the waiter two forks.

"Excuse me sir." The waiter walked toward Todd's table.

"Ladies room." Erin stood, and Rob nodded. It would be a good time to go before the dessert that she really didn't need arrived.

"What do you mean the card was declined!" Todd roared in the quiet room.

Erin snickered as she walked away, but she was sure there were others that were not maxed out.

Inside the plush bathroom the walls were lined with mirrors. Erin thought of the unisex bathroom at the store where she used to work. It was not like this. Stalls were on one side of the room behind a door. At the vanity table sat Todd's date. So, she had only gone to the bathroom after all. She sniffed, and Erin saw her wipe the blackened smudges where mascara had run.

Erin walked around the corner to the stalls. Don't get involved, she told herself. But when she returned the girl still sat at the line of mirrors. Erin sighed.

"Tough night?" she asked as she reapplied lip gloss.

The girl wiped her nose and stood. "No, I'm fine." And she walked out the door.

"Erin, when will you learn?" she chided herself and walked back to the table where Rob sat staring at the molten lava cake, waiting on her.

"I thought you said something small?"

"This is not the one I pointed at, but oh my God will you look at it?"

"Good thing this outfit is stretchy," Erin said with a sigh. And with forks poised, they both dove in.

Not a crumb of the cake remained, when overly stuffed they walked arm in arm out the door bundled in coats and scarves against the snow quickly becoming a blizzard. Across the street sat the brightly lit police car and the tow truck wrenching up the crumpled Alfa Romeo. The sports car had not fared so well in the weather. Todd stood yelling instructions at the man in the wrecker. The tow truck operator, his cigar in the corner of his mouth, ignored everything being hollered.

"Should we offer him a ride home?" Rob asked.

"No." Erin smiled and snuggled against Rob. He smiled back and pulled her closer. "He'll find his way home."

Todd's date—nowhere in sight.

"Still want to see that movie? I rented one before we left. I don't know if Mom is home or not, but she'll probably go to bed anyway."

"Sounds like a plan." Rob opened the door to the car and she climbed in.

Chapter 22

"Look, I know the kid can be a problem sometimes. You and I were the same when we were kids. He's young. But rape? Who does this girl think she is? Accusing my son of rape... He probably forgot to call her the next day or something. Or maybe she has a boyfriend or whatever. Rape? Stupid." Howard Newman sat across the desk from Nathan who had never seen the man so stressed. He tried to hide it, but his body language showed worry.

"Well the charges are there, and I can't undo them. I can, however, suggest a good criminal attorney." Nathan knew enough of Howard's dirty dealings in the world. But could Todd be a rapist? One way or another, the girl pressed charges. The charges stared him in the face in black and white on the Oklahoma Supreme Court Network. OSCN information was available on the internet for all to see. Some college girl that Todd picked up in a bar filed rape charges.

"I don't want some stranger, I want you. You've been the family attorney for a long time and I trust you."

Howard really trusted that Nathan could keep his mouth shut and help him sweep this under the rug. "Well, that's commendable but I don't handle criminal actions. You need a good criminal attorney and I know one. Someone who is used to Tulsa County and how things work around here; knows the judges and DAs. I'll give you a name, or I'll call him myself if you want me to. Like it or not—whether Todd did anything or not—he must face the music. The girl is entitled to her day in court." Nathan twirled a pencil searching the contact list on his computer.

"And I have to pay for it. Little twit! Where does she get off…?"

"Howard, that attitude will not get you where you want to go. You need to meet this head on and with professional help. I'm sorry it will cost you, but I don't think money is the problem here. I'm going to give Gary a call and then he can handle it from here on."

"Okay, but I want you in on it too. I want you to keep me apprised of the situation. Like I said, I don't want some stranger in my business."

"Well, that will cost you double, you know." Nathan knew Howard could pay the bill.

"I don't care. I have to protect my son, or his mom will have my hide."

Nathan doubted that Mrs. Newman had much to say about anything, and Howard wasn't afraid of her. Howard's problem centered around his own reputation and what this might do to it.

"Understood." Nathan punched in the phone number of his old college roommate who went into criminal instead of civil law like him.

****

"He's on OSCN." Nicole sat at the desk in her office staring into her computer screen. Erin walked in, papers in hand. Aside from Nicole, the office sat empty.

"Hi," Erin said. "Who's on OSCN?"

"That guy I told you about."

151

Erin thought about the pile of work back at the office. "I'm sorry what guy?"

Nicole looked stricken. "That Newman guy that I told you I went out with."

"Newman?" The cogs began to turn in her mind as she remembered the conversation in the bathroom at the library.

"Yea, Todd Newman." Nicole returned to the website of the Oklahoma Supreme Court Network. "You know I told you he tried to rape me?"

"You went out with Todd Newman?" Erin knew her face showed shock as she dropped the papers she had stacked in her hand. "Crap. They were in order," she said to no one.

"Yeah, do you know him?"

"Yeah, his family has a place at the lake and we went to school together." Thoughts of the prom resurfaced, and Erin shook her head to make them go away. "You didn't tell me who you went out with. We were interrupted when Jake came in."

"Is he a friend of yours?"

"No," Erin said more quickly than she intended.

"But you know him?"

"Yes, I know him. But I wouldn't call him a friend."

"Well, someone has filed rape charges against him." Nicole stared at the computer screen.

"Really? He raped someone? I heard about this in the bathroom at the library the other night but hadn't put it together." Erin leaned over the screen to read.

Nicole raised her head slowly. Her eyes were narrowed and ran up and down Erin. "He planned to rape me. I told you that. Did you not believe me?"

"Of course! I didn't mean that. It is just that..." Erin took a deep breath. "Todd and I have a history. He invited me to the senior prom and then humiliated me in front of the entire senior class. I thought of him as prince charming before we went out. Afterward, I knew better."

"Well, I met him at a frat party I went to with Jake, and he seemed like a nice guy. It never crossed my mind that I might end up in that position."

"Well, I should have known better than to go out with him. After all I had gone to school with him."

"I understand. Some guys think that because you got pregnant in high school you're easy pickins'. At least I guess that's what he thought."

"Jake asked me about you the other night at the library. He wanted to know why you wouldn't go out with him. I told him I didn't know."

"He's a good guy. I guess I'm just running scared right now." The girls bent over the computer screen once again—when Jake walked in the door.

"Hey ladies. Whatcha lookin' at?" He rounded the corner and leaned in to see the computer screen. "Hey, I know that guy. He goes to TU," he said after reading the screen. Both girls raised their heads, then Erin backed away.

"Nicole, can you get these Orders signed and give me a call? I'll pick them up later." She smiled at Jake and walked out the door. She didn't need to be in the middle of their conversation.

Chapter 23

"Dad, he has been accused of rape by a college student. And Nicole said he tried to rape her too. I see a trend here. I'm trying to get Nicole to file charges. I really need your help on this one." The footstool that normally sat in front of his mother's chair moved near his dad where he could sit on it. Dad, with his feet up in the recliner, folded the paper in his hand and gazed down at the son he loved deeply. They had a good relationship based on trust. Jake had a head on his shoulders.

"Jake, listen to me. Nicole must make this decision herself. None of us know what went on that night. Maybe they drank. Maybe Nicole, happy for the attention at first, changed her mind."

"Dad, no means no. You taught me that—taught me to respect girls. I'm not sure Todd had that upbringing. But one way or another, Nicole fears him and his family. She's devastated that this happened. She confided in a girl that works for Cronkite and Associates and then me—only because I stumbled into them talking. I really like her and want to help her out. What can I do to get her to stand up and take care of this?"

"Well the Newmans have a lot of money, and a lot of clout around here. Nicole has none. The Newmans can afford the best lawyer money can buy. Nicole knows that. She is a single mother living with her grandmother trying to make ends meet."

"You always taught me that everyone deserved justice, not just those who could afford it." Jake stared at his father. He breathed deeply. "I know the Newmans can buy anything they want, but if Todd is really doing this, he needs to be stopped. They don't need to be allowed to buy their way out of this one. And Nicole could help stop him from hurting someone else. Can you please talk to her?"

The judge sighed. "Okay, I can talk to her, but it might be a good idea if you were there too, or at least tell her I am going to bring up the subject. She is my bailiff and our relationship is different than the one the two of you have. It is obvious you like her and want to protect her. I do too. But just remember, this will be hard on her. She might have to testify if she brings charges and that could be difficult for her, her grandmother, and that little boy they are raising together."

"Thanks. I'll mention it to her. And then maybe we can talk to her together."

****

"Erin, can you come in here a minute?" In Erin's tiny office the screen on the telephone intercom said only "Cronkite." He needed to see her. Now that she had an office—it had once been a broom closet and barely had room for the desk—he called her a lot. They were working on the case again. The one he hated. Maybe hate was not the right term. He obsessed over the case. And these days she did too. They found the mother and resumed the paternity case against Karen Little a/k/a Samantha Smith.

Spring warmed up and summer drew near. Erin's first year of college almost over just in time for the trial, and naturally, just in time for finals. Erin had so many discovery materials to go over and organize she hardly had time to eat or sleep. They had to be in order and at the fingertips of the attorney when they went to court. But first, he had to decide which ones he needed the most.

After long days at the office, she still had class. She tried not to complain to Cronkite. And then one evening after she had eaten supper and come back to the office to finish some more work, he shook her awake at her tiny desk. Boxes were stacked on top of each other sitting on the floor and labeled with their contents. She had to climb over them to get to the chair. Her work now on a desktop computer that Erin backed up before she left at night. And took the flash drive with her. After the mess with the missing laptop—still not recovered—she found she didn't trust anyone at the firm but her aunt and Cronkite. Well, maybe Sara. And there were others that worked here that she cared for. They had been kind to her—all but Nathan and Stephanie. But she now felt she had to safeguard everything she worked on.

Erin walked down the hall to the open door of Cronkite's office. He sat behind the desk across from a woman with dark hair pulled back into a ponytail.

"Erin, I want you to meet—well, I guess you two already know each other." The woman turned and scowled. Erin could not believe her eyes. Sitting across from her boss she found Sally Elkman. And she didn't want to be there. Her angry expression attempted to be hidden by boredom. Erin knew Sally did not come of her own free will.

"Sally will be helping you with the discovery materials for the Dauber v. Little case. You need some help and she needs something to do. So, she will be working for Cronkite and Associates temporarily. She is here to work off a bill she owes, and her mother shouldn't have to pay for her. Isn't that right, Sally?"

Sally nodded her teeth clenched together.

"Erin, get the dolly and take the latest discovery materials to the conference room and show Sally how we bates-stamp electronically. Then you two ladies should be able to get that work taken care of in half the time." Cronkite picked up his phone, and with a wave of his hand, they were dismissed.

Sally stared at the girl she used to bully in high school and Erin almost managed to suppress a smile. The tables had turned.

"This way." Erin led Sally to the closet that held the dollies. Grabbing one, she pulled it back to the tiny office with the boxes of discovery materials.

"Okay, we have discovery materials for a case we are working on and we have to scan them in. The software will automatically bates-stamp them by giving them each a number and chart them in order, so we have a list of what we've received. We don't have to use the actual hand-held document stamp. I've been working on them for a while, so it will pick up with the next available number." Sally stood with one hip thrust out and her hand resting on it. She said nothing.

"Grab that box and we'll stack them on top of the dolly. Let's make as few trips as possible."

Sally still stood with her hand on her hip not moving. They stared at each other.

Erin breathed deeply. It would be impossible to deal with her. "Listen." Erin regarded at the girl in front of her. "I know we don't like each other. At least we didn't in high school. But this isn't high school. This case could be the difference between life and death for a little boy."

Sally snorted.

Erin continued. "His mother took him away from his father and hid him. We finally found her, and Mr. Cronkite wants justice for the dad and the boy."

Sally's stance softened slightly. "Well, if she took him from his dad, the dad had to be mean to them or something." Sally glanced at her nails.

"Sometimes that's how it goes. However, the mother is the nut case in this situation. She took the boy just to get back at the father. She has dragged the boy all over the country and changed his name. The child will never have a normal life if she is not stopped."

"How did you get in on this case? What makes you so special to Cronkite? And why were you running around with him at night bailing people out of jail?" Sally flipped her pony tail and then considered Erin.

Erin seethed. "I work for Cronkite. I wasn't running around with him at night. My aunt is a partner in this law firm and she helped me get this job. Cronkite knows I am going to school to become a lawyer and he is taking me under his wing. You don't have to like it. You just have to do the job that is paying off your attorney fees." By the time she finished Erin could feel her face burning.

"Grab the box and come on!" Erin stomped down the hall with the dolly letting Sally tote the last box by herself.

"First, I'll show you how to scan the documents, then we will print them out with the document number on them and place them into discovery notebooks to be used in court."

Erin and Sally worked into the afternoon and slowly Sally began to warm up. They would never be best friends, but Sally showed intelligence, Erin had not seen before.

"How's it going in here?" Cronkite stood in the door. He appeared silently as usual.

"We're fine." Erin glanced at Sally who nodded her head in response.

"Erin, I'll need three notebooks; one for me, opposing counsel, and the judge. But let me examine the document list first before we print the extra copies. We won't use everything. So, find some bank boxes for the original documents we don't use in court and three-inch binders for the ones we do. They will be in the basement with the extra office supplies. Email the documents you just scanned to me and I'll decide which ones we want in the books. If you don't find the office supplies you need, have Stephanie order it. Here, I also need these old files pulled while you are down there." He handed her a note with the files' names printed on it. "Bring them to me when you come back up, please."

Erin nodded.

"I'll show you how to email from the copier and then we can check out the basement. I've never gone down there, but Stephanie has the key." Sally appeared bored again when Erin mentioned a trip to the basement. "I'm sure it is lovely down there."

The elevator door opened to an area of the building Erin never ventured into. To the right appeared another door and Stephanie opened it with the key.

"Okay, office supplies are over there against that wall and Cronkite's closed files are the other way. Here's the flashlight and key." She pulled the string to the overhead lightbulb that swayed in the shadows with an evil look.

"I need those back when you're finished, so don't lose them." Stephanie stepped back inside the elevator and the doors closed.

"Nice." Sally's eyes were huge.

Erin considered the dark basement and sighed in resignation. No time like the present. "Let's get the office supplies first."

"If there are rats, I'm leaving. In fact, if there are mice, I'm leaving. I don't recall being told anything about working in a dungeon." Sally gazed around the room with disgust at cobwebs holding the shelves of closed files together. The smell of mold permeated the darkness.

"I'm sure there are no mice. If there were, the files would be eaten. They probably spray for rodents. Hopefully. Anyway, let's get the office supplies and then search for these files."

Sally stood with her arms folded over her chest and stared off into the darkness while Erin dug through boxes on the floor. The binders were easy to find as well as the exhibit tabs. Erin stacked a carton on the dolly. The leftovers could go in the supply closet upstairs. The closed files might take a bit more work.

"Okay, bring the flashlight over here and let's hope the files are in order. I have the list." Erin peeked back at Sally standing stock-still in the basement. The girl had probably never been dirty in her life.

"Sally, you coming? I need a light."

Sally moved toward the dark area of the closed files with the flashlight in front of her like a weapon, ready to swing at whatever came her way.

Erin ran her hand down the yellow, crumbling file labels holding the light from her cell phone in front of her for assistance. At least they were in order. The first two boxes of files were added to the dolly and Erin squeezed down the narrow pathway toward the last one.

At the end of the row she shined the light on the box she needed, but there were empty boxes on the floor in front of the shelves. Erin picked them up tossing them out of the way. The last box, heavier than the first, and when she tossed it something inside moved. A squeak and scratching noises sent shivers down Erin's spine and she threw the box as far as she could, bouncing it off the wall at the end of the row. She ran, bumping into Sally, who still stood holding the flashlight at arms-length. Erin tripped over something that spilled from the bottom shelf and she fell on her knees. She didn't know if she screamed or if Sally did, but a scream echoed in the basement. It may have been the only thing they ever did in unison.

There on the floor shining in the light of a flashlight lay the lost laptop. Hidden in plain sight in and among Cronkite's closed files, under L for laptop— sure to be found eventually. She picked it up and turned it over. The ding on the top of the silver case still there. She opened its lid to find the "E" and "S" keys rubbed off from use. Yes, she found the laptop she used before she had an office.

"A laptop? Down here?" Sally stood close behind Erin with the flashlight pointed at the computer. "This moisture can't be good for a computer."

"It used to be mine—at least until someone stole it." Erin knew immediately she said too much when she observed Sally's face.

"Stolen? From where?" Sally stared at the computer in Erin's hands.

"I'd been using it on this case and it turned up missing. I back up my work on a flash drive at night and take it home with me."

"Who would steal your work?

"That is a good question." Erin eyed the box at the end of the row and knew she had to take it back with her—or come back later. "Whatever lived in the box is probably gone now. Right?" She shuddered, straightened her shoulders, and walked back to the end of the row. She pulled the box off the shelf. "Okay that's the last of them. Let's get these back upstairs."

"And mention to maintenance there is a rodent problem down here." Sally pushed the hand truck next to Erin to put the final box in place.

Chapter 24

Bo Mitchell, Assistant District Attorney for Tulsa County, walked in the door of Nicole's office early Monday morning—and smiled a weary smile. Nicole smiled back.

"Good morning, Mr. Mitchell." He often had conferences with the judge and visited his office.

"Good morning, Nicole." He stepped to her desk.

"The judge isn't in right now. Would you like to leave a message?"

"I'm not here to see the judge. I'm here to see you." He cleared his throat, paused, and wiped a hand over his mouth. "Judge Hardridge says you want to file charges against Todd Newman?"

Nicole quickly glanced around to see if anyone heard. Alone in the office when the DA came in, who would hear? Why did she feel so guilty?

"I, well, yes, I guess so."

"Relax, Nicole. Judge Hardridge spoke to me after the two of you talked. I thought it might be easier if I came to you since we both worked in the same building."

"This is all so new to me. I don't even know where to start. And I must admit, I'm a little nervous." Nicole toyed with pen in her hand.

"Don't be nervous. If what you say is true, a crime has been committed here."

"I don't lie." Nicole eyed the DA from across her desk.

"I didn't mean that you do. I guess that is just a hazard of the job, questioning everyone and everything. Can I sit down?"

"Of course, I'm sorry." Nicole gestured to the chair that sat in the corner near the cabinet. Mostly piled with paperwork that needed to be filed. Today it sat empty.

Bo leaned forward and stared deeply into Nicole's eyes. "Okay, to start with, tell me your side of the story."

Nicole stammered at first thinking of where to begin. She took a deep breath. "I went out with Todd because he seemed like a nice enough guy."

"Where did you meet him?" Bo crossed his legs and loosened his tie. He held a notebook on his lap with a pen ready to take notes.

"I met him at a frat party I went to with someone else." The DA raised his head. "He asked for my number and I gave it to him. Is this all really necessary?" Nicole fingered the pen on her desk and pulled on her skirt.

"Don't get stressed. These are questions the defense attorney will be asking, so you might as well get used to them. It might appear you date a lot of guys—going to a party with one only to give your number to another."

"I wasn't dating anyone at the time I gave my number to Todd. I went to the party with Jake and we were just friends."

The DA scribbled in his notebook.

"Okay, so when did Todd call you? I assume he used the phone number you gave him?"

"Yes. He tried to take me home that night, but I really didn't know Todd that well, so I said no. I came with Jake Hardridge and thought I should leave with him. After I got home that night, Todd called me. I thought it cute that he called me so fast, like he really liked me or something."

"So, you were impressed at first with Todd?"

"Yes, at first. He took me to a really nice restaurant and then we drove around the lake in his convertible."

"Then what happened?" He stifled a yawn. "Is that coffee I smell? I'm running late this morning and haven't had any. I apologize, I'm still little fuzzy and it smells really good." The DA eyeballed the room for the coffee pot.

"Of course, I should have offered." Nicole rose and crossed the room to the pot that had just finished dripping and filled two cups. "Cream? Sugar?"

"No, black is fine, thanks. So, then what happened?"

Nicole stirred cream into her own cup and crossed the room to her desk handing the DA his drink.

"We stopped at this place off the road where you could see the lake. The weather perfect and the tree frogs singing; I commented on the lake and how smooth it appeared. Suddenly, he just pounced on me." Her hands began to shake, and she sat the cup on the desk, holding them together hoping it would end the tremors.

"We can stop if you need to." The DA sat his coffee on the edge of the file cabinet above him and wrote a short note on his pad.

"No, that's okay. I need to get this out in the open. I have to say, it would be easier telling a woman."

"I understand. But you need to be sure you can do this. There will be questions in open court like this and you must come across as certain of what happened. Todd will be there scrutinizing you when you confront him. But I'll be there too and other people that are on your side."

Nicole sighed, took a deep breath, and continued. "I can do this. I have to do this. He needs to be stopped. I'm not the only girl he has done this to."

"Another has come forward. I understand you saw that on OSCN?"

"Yes, I've been searching the database. I heard the rumor that he had been charged, so I checked to be sure."

"So, what happened after he pounced on you?" Mitchell sipped the dark, hot liquid.

"He grabbed me and pulled at my blouse. I had dressed up that night for the date because I knew we were going out to eat. I know the Newmans have a lot of money, so I assumed we would go to a nice restaurant. Anyway, I had on a skirt and blouse and some new heels I hadn't worn before. I got out of the car to get away, but he came after me and threw me over the back of the car pulling at my…" She stifled a sob and took a deep breath. "He tried to pull off my panties." She stared down at her hands that were now laced together and squeezed until the knuckles were white.

"Go on." The DA made notes in the book he brought with him.

"I got away and ran down the road. Then he just got back in the car and took off the opposite direction. I walked all the way home in a torn blouse and new

166

heels. I had blisters on my feet by the time I came in the door. I told my grandma and she said the Newmans had always been rich and thought they could do what they wanted. She said I was lucky to have gotten away." Tears that had been brimming at the edge of her lashes finally spilled down her cheeks and she sniffed reaching for a tissue.

"So that's it? He grabbed you and tried to take your clothes off?"

"That's enough!"

"Of course, I didn't mean it that way. It must have been traumatic. But aside from blisters and a torn blouse there were no injuries?"

"No." Nicole had unlaced her fingers and rubbed the tense digits.

"Do you still have the blouse?"

"Yes, it is in the closet. I've been meaning to see if I could fix it, but I just don't want to wear it anymore. It carries bad memories." She blew her nose and reached for another tissue, throwing the first in the trash.

"Okay, don't get rid of it and don't fix it. We might use it as evidence."

The door opened and Judge Hardridge entered wearing his robe.

"Bo." He extended his hand to the District Attorney who had been talking to his bailiff.

"Judge. I've been talking to Nicole and we might have a case against Todd Newman that we can join to the existing one."

"Good. Good. Nicole, how do you feel about this?" The judge regarded his bailiff.

"I'm sure it is the right thing to do. I'm just a little nervous that's all. But Mr. Mitchell says he will be with me. I have to do this—even though it is hard." She dabbed at her eyes.

"You're a brave woman, Nicole, and anything that Jake and I can do to make things easier, you know we'll be by your side." The judge took off the robe he wore in court and hung it on the coat rack just inside his office door.

"Thank you, sir." Nicole stood holding on to the edge of her desk like a life raft. This would not be easy on her or her family. The Newmans were capable of anything or could pay someone to do the things they did not want to do. Todd had to be stopped before he hurt more people, but she had to think of her safety too, and that of her baby and grandmother.

Chapter 25

Poly Sci didn't hold much of a challenge for Erin—until today. Always interested in the subject, now she hated the class, and the things that went with it. Just seeing the text for class, left a bad taste in her mouth. She went back to work for the course book late that night and it caused her to run into Nathan and Stephanie in Cronkite's office.

Today she hated it for another reason. Today she had finals and she had to show up for class. She could not miss it if she wanted to pass the course. It also happened to be the first day of the trial for Dauber v Little. Of course, they fell on the same day. Oh, why not? The universe was obviously against her. She couldn't miss either one of them, but unless she cloned herself, she didn't know what she would do.

"You will just be late to the trial." Cronkite stood at the door to her office the night before when she explained her conflict. She knew a chance of a lifetime when she saw it—to sit at the lawyer's table before becoming a lawyer. Cronkite could have told her he would just take someone else to assist, but he didn't. "What time is the test?"

"Nine o'clock, same as the trial. I don't know what to do."

"I'll tell you what you are going to do. You are going to take the test, take your time, and ace it. Then you can meet me at the courtroom. Just come in as quietly as possible and pick up where we are. You've done a fantastic job with the exhibits. I'll have no trouble finding them until you get there. Just sit down when you do arrive and begin to take notes and give me the exhibits as I offer them into evidence."

"That's okay, for me to come in late?"

"We do what we have to do. Mr. Dauber will be at the table with me. We'll be sure to have plenty of notebooks and pens. He and I will transport the documents to the courthouse, and you meet us when you get through."

Erin had no idea how she had landed a job with such a supportive boss. But she would not let him down.

Driving home she continued to think about the opportunity she had been given and wondered if there would be a spot for her at Cronkite and Associates when she passed the Bar, if she passed the Bar. No, when. She would think positively.

"Hi, Mom." Erin unlocked her dorm room with the phone against her ear. "Just checking in with you. How are you?" Erin could hear the TV in the background and someone call, "want more pizza?"

"Hi sweetie, I'm fine. You ready for finals in the morning?"

"Yeah. You having a party? Who's there?"

"Just Brent. He brought over pizza and we're getting ready to watch a movie."

"You guys are seeing a lot of each other these days." Erin tossed her books on the bed.

"Some yes. When did you say the first day of that big trial was?"

"Tomorrow." Erin could hear her mother take a drink and swallow.

"No, wait, I thought finals were tomorrow."

"They are. And they both start at nine o'clock." Erin glanced around the room. No roommate. Good, she would be able to study.

"What are you going to do? You can't miss the final."

"No, Mr. Cronkite said I could come in late. So, I'll take the test and then go to court."

"You are really busy and I'm glad you decided to move to Tulsa. Of course, I miss you, but going from high school and a weekend job at a flower shop to college and a courtroom; I don't know how you do it. By the way, Brent says hi."

"Hi back. The change is a challenge, but I love it. It is exactly what I want to do."

"Well, don't work too hard and get some studying done. Maybe we can get together this weekend and go shopping. Maybe have a girl's lunch or something."

"That sounds great. It will be a busy week, and I'll need to relax by then. Talk to you later, Good night. Love you."

"Love you too, sweetie." Erin could hear her mom click off the phone.

She walked in the door of the classroom dressed in the suit her aunt gave her. It seemed odd to go to class dressed up, but she had somewhere to be afterward. Students watched her when she walked in with clicking heels. She might never learn to run in them like Janice, but they went with the outfit.

The test proved easy. And that made her nervous. Political Science, the basis of a law degree, was also the basis of the LSAT test. She studied hard the night before even though she knew she could pass it. Erin sat down poised and ready—as ready as she would ever be—and scanned the questions. Easy. All things in life should be this easy, like schedules. She checked the answers off in her mind as she read and then returned to the top and began in earnest.

Erin finished much too quickly, and she scanned the test again. She had to pass this test. She glanced around the room at students with their heads down worrying over the final exam and breathed deeply. Then she turned in the test and ran for the car. She turned in the direction of the courthouse. Life—a non-stop whirlwind.

Tiptoeing in the courtroom, she pushed the squeaky gate that opened from the gallery to the table sitting at the front of the room. She walked quietly to the table and pulled out the chair. It too squeaked. All eyes were on her. She sat as quietly as possible. The defendant's attorney stood speaking, eyes boring into her as she sat. Cronkite nodded, scribbled something on a piece of paper and slid it in front of her. It read: "*Ace it?*" She nodded. He crumpled the paper loudly and smiled.

The case dragged on into the morning with expert witnesses and evidence on both sides, and finally broke for lunch. Erin took notes to give to Cronkite afterward. There might be questions.

"Erin, go get us some lunch and then meet us back here." Cronkite handed her a wad of cash from his billfold. "Mr. Dauber and I have some things to discuss so we'll stay here." The opposing counsel's table quickly cleared, and the judge already gone.

"What do you want?"

"It doesn't matter just get three of them."

Erin ran to the car thinking of a close drive-through. There were sandwich shops downtown, but she would have to wait in line. She hoped she chose the fastest way as she drove away. Tapping her fingers on the steering wheel, she waited in the drive-through line impatiently, finally given her order.

Walking back into the courtroom, she toted a drink holder and bag of burgers. Cronkite and Dauber talked in hushed tones still at the table.

"That was fast." Cronkite stood and took the drink she handed him.

"I hope hamburger and fries are okay for everyone." Erin handed the burgers around and the extra napkins she asked for at the window. They didn't need grease on the paperwork.

"It's fine, Erin. Whatever you came up with smells great." He smiled at her. "It will smell like burgers in here the rest of the day."

"Oh, I didn't think of that. I just wanted something fast. I hope it is okay with the judge that it smells like fast food now."

"Don't worry about it. No one will care—except maybe opposing counsel who happens to be a vegetarian. He'll complain, but who cares. Maybe it will knock him off his game."

"Oh no," Erin groaned. Cronkite let out a lusty laugh as he launched into his greasy burger.

Erin read over her notes while eating with one hand, then cleaned up the trash just before everyone began to trickle back in. Opposing counsel's nose twitched immediately and he glared at Erin's table.

"All rise," the clerk called as the judge walked in and sat down.

"Your Honor, I want to complain about the pungent odor of fried meat in the courtroom today."

"Smells good—did you get fries with that, Cronkite?"

"Yes, Your Honor." Cronkite grinned.

"Let's proceed." The judge placed his glasses on and picked up the paperwork in front of him.

The opposing counsel sat down heavily and began thumping his pen against the table.

"Your Honor, we would like to present our exhibit of the petition filed by the mother—while a resident in another state—to terminate the father's parental rights." Cronkite handed the exhibit to the judge and opposing council. "My assistant prepared a chart showing the trek the mother took while on the run with the child." He handed a copy of Erin's spreadsheet to both parties. The judge considered it holding his hand up for silence while he read.

"And Mr. Cronkite, these addresses and dates correspond to the affidavits attached to the spreadsheet?" The judge began to see things their way.

"Yes, Your Honor. They are the result of searches that found people who knew them."

Karen Little's attorney tried to object, but the judge did not allow it. Erin's spreadsheet stood up in court.

The afternoon shadows from the sun streaming in the window became longer as the day wore on.

The judge yawned and stretched. The courthouse closed at 5:00. "Let's resume this at 9:00 in the morning and Mr. Cronkite, maybe something less pungent for lunch tomorrow?" The judge began gathering up his paperwork.

"Yes, Your Honor." Cronkite tried unsuccessfully to hide a grin.

"We are adjourned." The judge banged his gavel and left the bench. Erin packed up the discovery documents and placed them back in the cart to pull to the office.

"Well, I think that went well." Cronkite nodded at Erin after they returned to the office. After five o'clock the office was almost empty. The music of the one CD owned by Erin's co-worker shut down suddenly and the light in that area clicked off. Cronkite pulled a bottle of brown liquid from the bottom desk drawer and two glasses from the cabinet behind him.

"Celebratory drink?" He nodded to Mr. Dauber. "Our efficient assistant can't join us, she is too young, and I don't want to go to jail for contributing to the delinquency of a minor, so she'll have to grab something from the kitchen." He nodded to her.

Erin grabbed snacks in the kitchen and a drink from the refrigerator, then ran back to Cronkite's office. She tossed cookies and crackers in the center of the round table and they were picked up and nibbled. It had been a long day.

It was the first time since she woke up today that she relaxed, and exhaustion over took Erin. Thankfully she only had to drive back to the dorm, not her mother's home in Mannford. She yawned and smiled. She felt a deep sense of accomplishment being a part of a case that could save the boy and his father. At least she hoped it would.

"Tired, little girl?" Cronkite smiled at her. "I'm sorry. You are not a little girl anymore, not the way you have performed on this case."

"Thank you." She smiled a sleepy smile and stretched. "Do you need me anymore this evening? I'll be in early in the morning."

"No, just get a good night's sleep. And Erin, great job today. Your chart was right on point and may be what wins us this trial." Cronkite smiled at her again as she walked from the room. "She's going to make a great attorney someday," she heard him say as she walked away.

The trial began again at nine o'clock the next morning. Erin arrived at seven. She checked and rechecked the exhibits making sure they were all there even if they had already been admitted into evidence. They might be needed again.

Mr. Dauber spent most of the morning staring at his ex-wife as she attempted to avoid his gaze. Dressed in a broomstick skirt and blouse with messy hair pulled back into a clip. She might have once been an attractive woman, but the years had not been kind to her. Possibly, the lies and deceit had taken their toll.

Both sides rested before closing arguments. The opposing counsel had little to say in closing as the late afternoon sun spilled through the windows. Shadows played on the walls as clouds floated overhead. The day would soon be done.

Cronkite stood, glanced down at his notes, and cleared his throat. "Your Honor, the defendant took the child from his father after the court ordered joint custody. She then willfully and maliciously towed the child from state to state, not only keeping him from the father he knew and loved but changing his identity so many times he had no idea who he had become. She essentially brainwashed him and lied about the whereabouts of his father. She fed him lies daily until the child no longer knew the truth about anything. The boy will need years of therapy to get over what his mother did to him; all to get back at the father for the divorce. She cared little for the child, but only for herself and the vengeance she sought against his father. It is our plea that the mother's parental rights be revoked, and the child be placed in the sole custody of the father who has spent the last five years of his life, and his life savings, trying to get his son back." Cronkite soaked with sweat, sat down. He glanced at Erin and she knew they had done a good job and hoped justice would play out in favor of the client. He had been through enough. But the court would make the final decision.

The mother stared off into space as Cronkite spoke trying to avoid locking eyes with the child's father. Maybe she planned her next escape.

The judge stared out over his glasses and spoke. "This case has been unusual as well as gut wrenching. I am happy to say I've seen few this heinous regarding a child's welfare. In the eyes of this court, the mother shows no remorse for taking the child from his father and turning the boy against him. And it is the finding of this court to agree with the plaintiff's plea to terminate the mother's parental rights and give the father sole custody their son." The gavel came down with an echo.

The courtroom sat deathly quiet until Karen Little cried out in pain—that appeared genuine. She had lost the child to his father. Erin almost felt sorry for her.

The mother, led from the courtroom in tears by her attorney, as the father glanced around anxiously for his son. He would be waiting with the DHS representative. They had won, and the boy could resume a normal life again. Erin wondered how disturbed the child would be after all he had been·through but knew the father would do his best to take care of him.

She scribbled notes as the judge spoke. Cronkite would need them to be typed in an Order for the judge's signature giving the father back his son. Lives had been changed that day, hopefully for the better.

And Erin had survived her first courtroom appearance.

## Chapter 26

The cherry-red Lexus pulled into the parking lot of the luxury hotel. The women were celebrating.

"I think they start serving brunch about ten thirty and there are mimosas for those who are so inclined." Toni winked at her sister. "Come on ladies it's party time!" Toni danced her way to the door. The other women lagged behind. Bernadette stood in the parking lot and stared up at the tower. Erin could hear Toni talk about the hotel all the way there. The spa was to die for she said, and the buffet divine.

"Close your mouth, flies will get in." Erin nudged her friend and pulled her along to the door.

"What flies? A place like this does not have flies. They couldn't afford to be here. I probably can't even afford the tip."

"That's what Aunt Toni is for. She said Cronkite was paying today." Erin smiled at her best friend, as her mother and Aunt Toni giggled about something when they entered the door.

"What do you think this will cost them?" Bernadette brushed her hair back from her face.

"Are you girls coming?" Alice stuck her head back out the door and called to her daughter.

Erin waved at her mother. "I don't know but they have the money. At least I hope they do or we'll have to take up a collection. After all, she said we were celebrating my first win in the courtroom—not that I won anything—I just sat at the table and took notes. And we both survived finals." Erin tugged on Bernadette's elbow.

"I may change my major to law," Bernadette said in awe and followed them in the door.

"First stop is the ladies' room." Aunt Toni walked purposefully to the elegant bathroom next to the fountain.

Standing in the kitchen after winning the Dauber v Little case that week, and completing finals for the year, Toni told Erin that they were going out for brunch and a spa date at a fancy Tulsa hotel she frequented. She had earned it, she said. Cronkite, instantly and quietly appeared as always. He never missed anything.

"A spa date? That sounds like fun. You ladies spare no expense. I'll take care of it." He winked at Erin.

Then the couple became a foursome; Toni, Erin, her mother, Alice, and Erin's best friend Bernadette. After all, how could she celebrate without her best friends and mother?

Toni walked away from the desk to the couches where the others sat. "Okay, the buffet does not open until eleven o'clock and we don't have spa treatments until one. So, Alice, I suggest a martini." She gestured the opposite way toward an opening that held the bar.

"At ten thirty in the morning?" Alice eyed her sister and then observed the elegantly furnished lobby once more. The fountain in the middle of the room reflected a rainbow of colors in its light show.

"Why not, we're on vacation, remember? You left your assistant in charge. Girls, you can't come in the bar, but there are tables right near the door. Order what you want." Toni nudged Alice to the bar and the two older women sat down.

"I still can't believe this place." Bernadette continued to gaze around the room. "What do you think the spa will be like if this is the lobby?" She ordered a soft drink from the attentive waiter and Erin told him to put it on the tab of the ladies at the bar.

Erin stared at the buffet. She filled her plate with delicacies of fruit and omelet, and then spied the muffins.

"I'll have iced tea," she told the waitress.

"Well, I'm having a mimosa," Aunt Toni chimed in. "Alice?"

"Well where I come from, Champagne is not a breakfast food. But why not, we're on vacation!" Erin had never seen her mother smile so broadly. But then again, aside from camping, Erin and her mother never vacationed.

The spa sat on the second floor. The frosted double doors let in plenty of light while providing privacy. Pulling them open Erin was immediately hit by the soft scents of lavender, eucalyptus, and mint. They took seats as Toni approached the counter to check on their reservations. No one spoke. The music played softly. Loud noises were not allowed.

"If you ladies will follow me, you can change in here and the lockers are on the wall. Leave your valuables in the locker and take the key with you. You will find towels, robes, and slippers for everyone. Once you are ready, come outside and wait in the sitting area. Your masseuse will be with your shortly. There are cold bottles of water in the cooler and it is suggested you drink plenty of it, so you won't get dehydrated. Massages can do that to you." The woman in pink scrubs with the name of the hotel embroidered on the front smiled as she gave them instructions.

"I want her job," Bernadette said. "In a place that caters to making other people feel relaxed and comfortable. What a way to spend your day."

Erin and Bernadette stood in the middle of the room in awe. The scent of lavender stronger there.

"Come on girls, you heard the lady, get undressed and ready." Aunt Toni pulled her top over her head and reached for the robe.

"Aunt Toni, I've never done this before. Do I take off everything?" Erin glanced at her mother who also appeared worried.

"You don't have to, honey, leave on your panties if you want, but the bra probably needs to go. No one is going to touch anything they shouldn't, but they will be massaging your back and the straps will get in the way." Toni patted Erin on the shoulder reassuringly.

Alice and Bernadette both sighed in relief.

They waited in fluffy robes and slippers with bottled water until four masseuses arrived. The four women were led down the hall to separate rooms that were dark and warm with music playing in the background.

"You girls have a good time and holler if you need anything." Toni winked again as she entered the door. "Not that I'll be able to get up."

"First massage?" The young masseuse helped Erin lay face down on the table with the sheet over her.

Erin nodded feeling apprehensive. But the food she had eaten, and atmosphere soon put her into a stupor.

"Okay, I'll start with the arms, then, legs, and then back. You tell me if I am too rough or too light. The heated table will help you relax as well as the rhythm of the music. I want you to have a good time and enjoy the hour we have together."

"An hour?" Erin didn't know if she could lay still that long.

"Believe me, it will be over much too soon. I know, I have them myself. If I do my job right, you will emerge relaxed and drowsy."

An hour later, Erin stepped out of the massage room with her hair in disarray. She saw her mother walking off down the hall in the wrong direction, her masseuse calling her back. She had a sleepy smile on her face. "Oh my God. Why have I not been doing that for years?" Alice swept her hair from her face.

Given more water they were led to the steam room. When the door opened a thick cloud of steam escaped enveloping them as they stood in front of it.

"This is the best place in the world to shave your legs, ladies." Aunt Toni pulled out a razor and small bottle of baby oil. Her robe on the hook, she wrapped in a towel with another on her head and sat on the wooden seats. Alice sat down beside her sister.

Erin and Bernadette walked to the other side of the tiny room still drowsy and sat on the redwood benches. Bernadette coughed several times. "I feel like I'm drowning," she said.

"Breath deep, honey." Toni took in a deep breath and let it out slowly. "You don't want to mess up that buzz you have going from the massage. And ladies take off the robes. You'll burn up. There are towels. Let the steam open up those pores and cleanse you. Are you

183

having a good time?"

Both girls nodded.

Alice grabbed towels for everyone and quickly hung her robe up. "Toni, you know I have never had a massage?" Her hair hung in her face and there were smudges under her eyes where mascara ran down her face.

"Really? How about you girls, virgins to the massage parlor too?"

They both nodded again.

"Well, soak it in ladies. I have to report back to N. Robert that we spent his money well." Toni propped one leg up to shave it.

Erin wrapped in a towel and handed one to Bernadette who still appeared unsure. She turned around and dropped the robe and wrapped in the towel given to her. Then followed her friend.

"You'd think they could at least have bigger towels," she said sighing and trying to hold the edges together.

Toni erupted in laughter. "Oh honey, those double Ds will never fit in that. It is meant for your hair! Get the bigger ones on the shelf."

Giggling like school girls, they passed the baby oil around, and then the razor.

"I don't know how sanitary it is to share a razor, but at least we will all come out with open pores, relaxed, and fuzz-free." Toni poured more water on the stones and a thick layer of steam instantly filled the room. The women giggled and chatted, finally comfortable with the lack of clothing. Erin had never been so relaxed and carefree in a room full of people with no clothes—and clouds of steam.

The door to the steam room opened and a young woman with dark hair stood in the doorway. She glanced around—then quickly left closing the door behind her.

Erin stared at Bernadette. "Was that Sally?"

"I hope not. Way to ruin a mood." Bernadette giggled, stood, and walked to the door. "I'm cooked, and my curls are worse than normal. I've had all the luxury I can stand for one day. Time for a shower."

"Well, not me. I could stand this forever, but if the party is moving, so will I." Toni dropped her towel and reached for the robe once again and they all left the steam room together. The brightly lit locker room hit Erin's eyes bringing her back to reality.

"Ladies there is fabulous shampoo and toiletries in the showers. Be sure to use them and take home the leftovers. We've paid for them." Toni gestured to the showers as she stepped into the enclosure.

"We forgot the baby oil." Erin turned and walked back down the hall. She pulled open the door to the steam room and stepped inside. Sally stood naked at the back of the room. Even in the dark steam room, Sally obviously had massive bruising on her solar plexus. She instantly tried to cover herself with her arms and turned around without a sound.

"Sally? Are you okay? What is wrong with your stomach?" Erin stared at the nude woman trying to hide herself. "Are those bruises?"

"Go away." Sally took a step farther to the back of the tiny room.

Erin reached for her shoulder, but found it too bruised to touch. Sally had bullied her in high school, but she was also the woman she'd had shared the horrors of the basement at work. She appeared to have been badly beaten.

"Sally, really are you okay?"

"I said go away, I'm fine." Sally gritted her teeth.

"Did someone hit you?" Although intruding, Erin felt the need to help.

Sally jerked away and grabbed the towel. "I'm fine and you didn't see anything. Now just go."

Erin stood with the bottle of baby oil in her hand and walked to the door. "If you need to talk, you know where I am most days." Erin walked out the door.

## Chapter 27

Sally couldn't sleep. She pulled the sheets loose from the bed she lay in for days as she twisted and turned. She might never leave her dorm room again. She dozed once or twice and woke up sweating trying to get away—or sometimes in her dreams she tried to rescue someone else. The dreams were confusing. She'd had enough sleep.

She had been raped. How could that happen to her? Could your boyfriend rape you when the two of you had sexual relations in the past? All she had were questions, and not answers. She knew two things for certain: she hurt all over and felt worthless. She went to the spa to try to relieve some of the physical pain and ran into someone who would probably talk. Would Erin tell people what she saw, that Sally could be weak enough to allow herself to be a victim. She had to hide this from everyone. And now Erin knew.

Groaning, she pulled on her baggiest jeans and a long-sleeved T-shirt. Overdressed for the summer heat, she didn't want any questions about the bruising. She just wanted to get out of the dorm and find some coffee. Coffee and a snack, and the student union had both. Hopefully, not many people would be there this time of day. Most of them were in the classes she skipped today.

Stepping away from the coffee machine, wearing a

hat and sunglasses indoors, she walked to the chairs on the other side of the room. She sat under the bulletin board covered with thumbtacked flyers hanging on the wall. The hot liquid burned her tongue. But the pain allowed her to feel alive. Not good, but alive. She opened the package of crackers pulled from the vending machine and munched. Her eyes were drawn to the flyer in the corner of the board. Counseling services were available to students. Would they tell anyone if she talked to them? They couldn't, could they? She had never felt so miserable as she sipped the coffee made in a vending machine. It was comforting but terrible—a lot like her relationship with Todd.

She walked to the door of the counseling center and opened it. She would make an appointment. Just to see what her options were. Maybe she could talk to someone who wouldn't tell the authorities. She couldn't continue her life this way.

****

Gary Hernandez waited in Nathan's office. From out of town with no office of his own, Nathan's would have to do. If this case took long, he would rent something downtown. But he didn't think it would. He already found some dirt on the local DA who filed the charges. His assistant checked every nook and cranny. They always had something hiding in the closet. No one could be pure as the driven snow.

The DA in Tulsa County had a son—a cancer survivor—and somehow the boy climbed the ladder for stem cell replacement shortly after his grandfather made a BIG contribution to the cancer research center. Good for Grandpa. And good for the kid, who lived. But he might not have without the money. Maybe the other patients would like to know how the boy moved up.

Hernandez knew the Newmans wouldn't mind a little snooping into the background of the DA. After all they hired him. If they wanted to win, they'd come to the right place. And he knew they wanted to win.

The door knob turned, and Nathan ushered in the overweight older man who obviously had a close relationship with the bottle by the looks of his nose crisscrossed with visible capillaries. Those were the best kind of clients. Predictable.

Hernandez stood and smiled.

"Gary Hernandez," he said stretching out his hand to the new client.

"Howard Newman, Mr. Hernandez. Nathan says you are the best, and you'd better be because this bullshit is costing me a lot of money."

"Well, I assure you it is money well spent. I've already dug up some dirt on your local DA and I think I can get the charges dropped with very little trouble."

"Blackmail in my own county, Gary?" Nathan raised an eyebrow.

"Trust me Nathan. Let's talk before anyone gets overly concerned." Gary smiled his practiced crocodile smile.

Nathan gestured to the back of the office where four chairs sat around a table big enough for small gatherings. Anything larger had to go to one of the conference rooms in the firm.

"I think this table will do for today. I didn't want to use one of the larger and more public conference rooms." Nathan's visitors sat.

Chapter 28

Todd woke up in a sweat, having the dream again—the one he had as a kid.

Always the same, he watched unable to move, as his father beat his mother senseless. Blood splattered over the room and his mother looked like a rag doll as he hit her mercilessly. Was she dead? Todd hid under the table with his brother's hand over his mouth to keep him from screaming. Why did she not fight back? To protect them, or because of weakness and fear of the old man? They all feared him.

But it was a dream, not reality. In reality the beatings never actually happened, not physically at least. Dad's tongue, sharper than any blade, packed a harder punch than any fist. *Sticks and stones may break my bones, but words will never hurt me.* That nursery rhyme did not hold true in Todd's household.

Maybe Mom got what she deserved. If you didn't stand up for yourself, the world would run you over. Todd learned that on the football field and it held true in life. The old man could be right, now and then. You made your own way in this world and if you didn't hit first, you would be the one who got hit.

He stood beside the bed and raked a hand through his hair. A shower might scrub away the feeling he got from the dream. He hated his Dad and all he stood for, and the dream happened more and more. He hoped that didn't mean he'd started to like it. That was sick. Too much to think about so early in the morning and he headed for the shower.

Hitting the road in the Alpha he ran through the gears as he raced around corners. Classes could wait. The weather had begun to cool but still he dropped the top. He knew a place in his hometown that used to be a racetrack. Paul Newman once raced there, but of course like all good things, it no longer existed. Well, it existed, but now it was a trailer park. He hugged the curve as fast as the Alpha would maneuver, tires squealing—and then she stood in the middle of the road. A little barefoot girl in a pink dress with a ragged bunny by the ear stood in the middle of the road. He swerved to the right and hit the brake sliding into the curve. She never moved. Her wide blue eyes stared at him, and he at her, through the windshield. Her lip trembled and sweat ran in his eyes. He wiped it away. In a flash she ran back up the rickety steps to the door that hung on crooked hinges and the safety her home provided. Who let their kid run around barefoot in the middle of a road in traffic?

"Damned kid!" The sweat again trickled down his face. Then it hit him. The only traffic on the concrete, buckled from years of neglect, was the Alpha. He caused the safety issue for the girl.

He gunned the engine and eased over the rough road. He didn't need to put the car back in the shop. The precious car, purchased on his own when his trust fund kicked in on his eighteenth birthday, had to be taken care of. Dad didn't like it, Mom hated it even more. She said he would die in it, but he loved the way it maneuvered in his hands. The oak steering wheel, made in Italy, handled even better at higher speeds. The car screamed for the open road—not swerving around hairpin turns with grass and abandoned trailers on either side. He gunned the engine and pulled out of the neighborhood headed for the highway, his hands slick with sweat on the steering wheel.

The old Highway 51, no longer in use, had been rerouted so that parts ended in the lake. Fisherman loved the area with the broken road. The fish did too. The new highway ran over the dam to other parts of the lake; parts with boat slips and floating restaurants that doubled as karaoke bars on the weekends. Sometimes a girl worked there, slinging drinks. Maybe Christine worked today.

He pulled the sports car into a parking spot between two pickups. Most boaters had pickups to pull their boats and there were a lot of boats in the slips, some in the marina for repairs. Sports cars seemed out of place here.

Walking down the gangplank he watched the ducks and heard children splashing in the water quickly cooling at the end of summer. No beach here, but it never stopped a kid who wanted to swim. He hoped these children were better supervised than the last one he encountered.

Todd had a friend with a sail boat who used to take him sailing. But friends were in short supply these days. He remembered being hit in the face with the rope when the boom slipped out of his friend's hands. They were in this cove and coming around slowly when it happened. He had a nasty shiner later. Thankfully only the rope hit him and not the boom or he would not be here to think about it today. He missed the lazy days of sailing this lake. Maybe he needed a sail boat—one of his own so he didn't have to rely on friends. Maybe he would sail the Caribbean and drop out of school. He could be a pirate. But he was too old for that type of fantasy.

He opened the door to the restaurant decorated in a nautical style. Country music greeted his ears.

"Christine working today?" he asked the guy behind the bar. Still too early for customers. The small weekday lunch crowd had not arrived.

"Tonight, I think," he grumbled around the stub of an unlit cigar.

"Okay, tell her Todd stopped by." He paused. "I'll have a Coke."

The man pulled the can of Coke from the ice and handed the dripping drink to him.

"That'll be three fifty."

"Damn, for one drink?" Todd pulled his billfold from his pocket and handed the man a five-dollar bill.

"Take it or leave it," the man said reaching for the money.

They stared at each other for several seconds. "Do I get my change?" Todd asked.

"That your sports car out there?"

"Yeah, it's mine." Todd observed the man whose eyes narrowed, then a slight smile crept near the corner with the cigar.

"Consider it a tip, Todd. I'll tell her you were by."

Todd knew she would never get the message. He shook his head over the fruitless trip and left the floating restaurant.

Near the Alpha he suddenly heard screams coming from the water.

"Help! My brother!"

A young boy stretched his arm out into the deeper water reaching for the other one.

Todd could see a small head go under just outside the reach of the larger one. The smaller boy slipped into dangerously deep water. Todd ran down the hill climbing over rocks that guarded the erosion of the bank and splashed through the water to the flailing boy and his frantic brother. Todd knew there were holes near the bank from all the years of propellers digging into the bottom. The little one had slipped under just out of reach of his brother and Todd grabbed a handful of water where he had last seen the boy's head. As he lunged forward again the boy's head reappeared, sputtering a mouthful of lake water. He grabbed the child's T-shirt and pulled him to shore, his brother right behind him.

"Dad!" The older boy ran to a man in rubber boots with jeans partially tucked into them and a dirty green baseball cap on his head.

"Hey! What chu doin' with my boy?" He ran at Todd snatching the child from his hands.

"Pulling him out of deep water. You need to watch them a little better." Todd wiped the water from his eyes.

The younger child continued to cough and gag while his older brother tugged at Dad's sleeve.

"He was drownded, Dad. He fell in a hole or sumthin'." The older boy's eyes were wide.

"That water's shallow. I been there a bunch a times," his father responded.

"It changes with the time of year."

The father quickly cut him off.

"You boys get on up there and get some lunch. Your momma's got food ready." He shoved the boys up the hill and turned to Todd. "Leave them boys alone, pervert."

Todd stared at the man for a moment. Dad could be right. Maybe you have to hit first or be hit. Shaking his head, he slogged up the hill to the Alpha, knowing it would be a wet drive home. He had no idea where the expensive can of Coke landed.

Chapter 29

The district attorney, sat at his desk inside the courthouse staring at his computer. He had to find a way to drop the charges against the Newman kid. The first charge of rape brought by some girl Newman picked up in the bar, seemed of little concern, a college student with student loans so high she would never see the light of day. The second—attempted rape—Newman didn't finalize the deal before she got away. At least that's what she said. She was Judge Hardridge's bailiff and that could be a problem. She didn't have a penny to her name either, but she had connections. The judge, known for being fair and decisive, wasn't up for re-election and he didn't have a lot of overturned decisions. A judge for the people according to the article in the Bar newsletter last year.

But unlike the victims, Todd Newman was represented by a criminal attorney brought in from out of town. The defense attorney had a reputation for being tough and just underhanded enough to get things done his way. He did his homework. He always found a weakness. And he had found Bo's—and threatened to use it against him.

Bo's son survived the bone cancer that ravaged his tiny body after he miraculously moved up the list of donors for stem cell replacement. The therapy didn't always work, but the oncologist thought little Bo Jr. had a chance if they could get him the treatment in time. Money from his grandfather to the cancer research center didn't hurt. Legal or not, Bo Jr. lived, and the research center had more money to work with. Problem? Bo knew what the problem was as he lay in bed at night tossing and turning thinking of the other patients waiting in line. Did they live? But, his only son survived. Now an out-of-town criminal attorney had dug deep enough to find out about the money under the table. He wouldn't mention it, he said, if the charges were dropped. However, it could be leaked to the press if they weren't.

When Bo took the job in the District Attorney's office he knew he would never be a millionaire. He worked for the state, and he sat in his cramped office working day and night to clean up the streets and protect the good people of Tulsa County. There were still good people out there. He believed that. He considered himself one of them until now. How had he been so stupid to allow his father-in-law to give the research a grant under the table? But then again, how could he stop him? And what if he had? Would Bo Jr. still be alive? A parent would do anything to assure that their child lived. No one could blame him for that; no one except maybe the parent of a child whose place in line got moved back. Did that child live? Too many questions. Just drop the charges and get on with the day. Sometimes you had to do what you had to do.

He stood up from his desk and reached for the phone.

Chapter 30

"Nicole, I can't believe this!" Erin stood at Nicole's desk as the girl once again wiped the tears from her eyes. "How could they just drop the charges?"

"DA Mitchell said there wasn't enough evidence."

"But two people came forward." Erin could not believe her ears. After everything Nicole had been through, now the charges were dropped in her case.

"I know." Nicole blew her nose.

"I think there are other women who have had problems with Todd before. Word gets around. One night in the bathroom at the library I overheard a conversation between some girls. They didn't say they were raped. But they said he was insistent."

"Well, what is the difference? I mean where does the law draw the line between being raped and being insistent on sex? I thought no meant no." Nicole reached for another tissue.

"It does to most people. But the Newmans have a different set of values. I wonder if we got more people to file charges, if yours could be reinstated." Erin shifted the load of papers in her hands knowing she needed to get back to the office with them.

"I don't know. I'm not sure it is worth it. It might just be a lot of trouble and heartache for nothing."

"I'll ask Aunt Toni. She will know what it will take to get these charges back on the books. Just because you have a lot of money shouldn't mean you have the right to do what you want to anyone you please." Erin squeezed Nicole's shoulder and then walked to the door. "Call me if you need to talk. And I'll see what Aunt Toni says." She walked out the door as Nicole nodded. Her phone rang, and she sniffed before she answered it.

Erin didn't know the girls in the bathroom she overheard talking about Todd last winter. But with classes resuming next week many of them would be back at the library again. She would hang out there as much as possible and try to talk to them.

Classes started in a week and Erin had reached her twenty-first birthday. A junior in college. Last year had flown by. One semester flowed into the next and another year gone. In the summer she worked full time at Cronkite's. It seemed unbelievable even to her. This year she could sit for the LSAT test and if she passed, begin law school next year. Life moved fast. She remembered every adult she ever knew saying that, but she didn't believe it. Now she did. And life whizzed past in a heartbeat.

****

Classes back in session, Erin spent as much time as possible at the library. Rob, still working at the library, hoped to be able to find a research job soon. His professors wanted him, they just needed grant money to be able to fund the job. Bernadette worked in the professor's office again and Steve went back to the sandwich shop. The three of them visited him at least once a week, ate a late dinner and then all left together. Erin hadn't completely lost track of her best friends, but they were all doubly busy these days with school and work.

Erin tried to move study time with Bernadette to the library in the evenings. She hoped to find the girls again that she overheard in the bathroom talking about Todd. They could be the key to getting the rape charges against Todd reinstated, assuming any of them wanted to join in. If not, they might know someone who would. Bernadette didn't mind the library if they could get a table and sometimes the guys joined them too.

Her text for Constitutional Law propped up in front of her, Erin sat at the library table. She tried to study, but mostly she watched people. The law of averages said that eventually one of those girls would show back up—if they were still students at TU.

"Hey ladies." Rob's lanky frame stood behind Erin and he leaned over planting a kiss on the top of her head. Erin smiled and patted the chair next to her.

"Hi, Rob," Erin spoke with detachment staring toward the bathroom.

"Rob." Bernadette glanced up and back down at her book. Calculus kicked her butt most of the time. Spreading his pile of books across the table, Rob took up much more than his share of room. Instinctively, Erin moved over. Then he placed a book on top of hers. She glanced up.

"Are you trying to be a pain?"

"Yes." He smiled and scooted closer.

"What is your problem?" Erin felt edgy today. She had not seen the girls since school started, and fall had arrived. She feared she never would again.

"No problem." He smiled again.

Erin put down the book. Evidently, he needed something. She might as well talk to him. "What?" she asked irritated.

"I got in," was all he said.

"Into what?" Erin gazed into his eyes and saw mischief. She didn't have time for his silliness today.

"Probably into trouble," Bernadette replied never even glancing up from her work.

"I got into the grant program in the Engineering department. I start Monday and I will no longer be working in the library. Some other schmuck can put the titles back on the shelf in the correct order. Not that they will stay that way for long."

"Oh, there she is!" Erin stood knocking over Rob's books in the process. "Sorry." She walked away. "Oh, and congrats," she whispered loudly from a distance.

Rob's eyes narrowed at the girl he called his girlfriend. "Congrats, Rob," he said in his best girly voice. "So happy for you. Way to go. Let's celebrate!" Rob sighed and slid down in to his seat.

"Way to go Rob, let's celebrate." Bernadette smiled. "Maybe I can get your old job since the Secretary from Hell has my number. You would not believe what she had me doing today."

"What?" Rob still appeared irritated at Erin as she walked down the hall.

"Well, I don't think the old bat has filed anything since 1950. The pages are so yellow you can barely read them. I told her about electronic filing and she snorted. Anyway, I'm filing. But, I guess it is a paycheck—a small one."

Two girls passed by the table and waved at Rob, one of them batting her eyelashes like they might take off flying. "Hi Rob!" They giggled in unison.

"Hi," he replied.

Bernadette snorted. "Obvious much?" She watched the girls walk away and shook her head.

Rob smiled, then he glanced at Erin as she talked to the women by the bathrooms. He slid back down into his chair and stared at the girls in the distance—then stacked his books and stood.

"See you later," he said to Bernadette.

"You leaving?"

"Yeah, tell Erin I said bye." He walked the opposite way to the back door and down the steps of the library out into the evening air.

"I think one of them will talk!" Erin trotted back to the table and sat down.

"Your boyfriend left." Bernadette glanced up from the Calculus book.

"Where'd he go?" Erin still glanced down the hall toward the bathroom.

"I don't know, but he seemed irritated."

"Well, he'll get over it. I think one of those girls will talk to the DA about her experience with Todd. This may not be over yet." Erin appeared triumphant.

"That's great. But I think you ticked off the man of your dreams by not being available to celebrate with him. You live and breathe that job of yours."

"It's important." Erin twisted her hair trying not to feel guilty.

"So is Rob's."

"I know, but his is just a job to pay for school. This is so much more." Erin again glanced at the girls in the distance.

"I really don't get you. Where do you get off thinking your job is so much more important than anyone else's? It's like I don't know you anymore."

Bernadette glared across the table at the girl she had been friends with since grade school.

"I don't think what I do is more important. But it is important to the women that Todd has hurt. I know your job is important too. And Rob's. But, I just feel I need to get Nicole some help with this charge. And those girls were right there. I had been waiting to see them since school started." Erin pushed the hair out of her face as she spoke.

"Well, tell that to the boyfriend who just walked out on you. He didn't seem happy."

"Like I said, he'll get over it." She hoped.

"You know you don't treat him very well sometimes. I mean if Steve ignored me when I had something important to say, I'd be pissed too." Bernadette returned to her book.

Erin's phone buzzed. The screen said "Toni." "Hi Aunt Toni!"

Bernadette peeked up from her book and placed her finger against her lips to shush her friend.

"I'm so glad you called." Erin spoke in hushed tones as she raced down the stairs and outside the building, so she could talk. "I think I have another girl who will come forward on the charges."

"That's great, hon. But I called for another reason. Have you talked to your Mom lately?"

"Yeah, we talk almost every day. Is everything okay?" Erin pushed open the library door and out into the evening air.

"Well you know she has had that cold, it moved into her chest and she sounds awful. You know how stubborn she is, and I thought you might talk her into going to the doctor."

"I didn't know it had gotten so bad. I just talked to her yesterday or the day before. I kinda lost track of time, I guess." Erin held the phone, so the wind did not blow into it.

"Well, you know how she is. I tried to convince her, but she won't listen to me. Maybe she'll listen to you."

"I'll call her. By the way, like I said, one of the girls I overheard in the bathroom came into the library tonight. I talked to her and she said she would discuss bringing charges with the DA." Erin still felt high about the encounter.

"That's great, hon. You getting any studying done? I don't want you so wrapped up in this job you neglect your studies." Aunt Toni sounded like a mother.

"I am, Aunt Toni. And I'll call Mom to check on her."

"Okay sweetie, I'll talk to you later." Toni clicked off her phone.

Turning around to go back to the library Erin ran right into Todd as he stepped out from behind the bush. He must have been listening by the knowing look on his face.

"Hey Erin." He smiled, and something about it reminded her of nails on a chalkboard setting her teeth on edge.

"Todd." She walked toward the door.

"Going somewhere?" He stepped in front of her.

"Back to the library where my friends are waiting." Erin stepped back and then stopped.

"What friends? I saw that boyfriend of yours leave a few minutes ago." The smile again.

"Are you watching me?" Erin could not believe

that he would admit to that.

"Maybe. You've been doing a lot of snooping around lately, talking to people you think you know and putting your nose into business that is not yours. It would be a shame to get that nose chopped off."

"I don't know what you are talking about." Erin took a step toward the safety of the library.

"You know the DA dropped those trumped-up charges. Now you won't leave it alone. You think you can get people to say things they shouldn't. Convince them of things that didn't happen. Why don't you just go away and live your life and let others live theirs?" His eyes were narrowed as he leaned closer.

"You raped a girl, Todd, and I am going to see to it that you are punished." Erin suddenly felt brave.

"That is my word against hers and the DA dropped the charges. I suggest you drop your interference into my life if you know what's good for you."

"You have to pay for the things you do in life, Todd."

He stepped forward until he almost touched her and then he stopped. "Just remember what I said. Stay out of it or you'll regret it. How's your mom, by the way? Did I hear you say she was sick? What a shame. I know you two are close. Remember what I said, or someone will get hurt." Todd walked around her and into the dark of the campus leaving Erin shaking.

Erin ran back into the library and up the stairs to the table where she and Bernadette studied. No Bernadette, only a pile of Erin's books. Well, two friends deserted her tonight just when she needed to talk to someone.

Picking up her books she left through another door

closer to her car. At least she had the good sense to park under a light she thought. Tossing her books in the backseat she headed for Mannford to check on Mom.

Chapter 31

"Mom?" Erin called as she walked in the back door of the house. Her mother's car sat in the driveway, but no one answered her call.

"Mom?" She walked down the hall to her mother's bedroom. She could see the bedside lamp on, but the bed empty. On the table sat some over-the-counter cold medicine. Back in the living room she saw an afghan and pillow wadded up at one end of the couch. Sitting down and picking up the pillow, she noticed its warmth. Mom must have just left—when her phone rang.

"Hi Mom, where are you?"

"Erin, this is Brent Taylor."

Erin paused. "Hi Brent. Is Mom okay?"

"That's why I'm calling. I have your mom's phone. She is at Hillcrest Medical Center in Tulsa. She passed out when she got up this evening and I took her straight here. She's in the emergency room and they may admit her. I used her phone to call you."

"I thought she had a cold." Erin, still in shock at the voice on her mother's phone. How long had it been since she had talked to her mom? The guilt began to creep in.

"Well, they think it might be viral pneumonia. They are going to run some tests. But it all happened fast. I stopped by to take her to get a burger, so she wouldn't cook, and when I got to the house, she was asleep on the couch. She got up to answer the door and barely made it. I guess this stuff really got her quickly." Brent's voice trembled with emotion.

"Okay, I'll be right there. I came home. It will take a few minutes to get back to Tulsa but I'm on my way. And Brent, thanks for taking care of my mom."

"You bet, kiddo, she is in good hands. You drive carefully."

"I will. And thanks again." Erin clicked off the phone and ran for the car.

She bounded through the emergency doors at the hospital as they automatically opened. Glancing around she found a woman behind the glass working the desk.

"I'm here for Alice Sampson." Erin leaned against the counter breathing heavily.

The woman searched her chart and then picked up the phone saying something to the person on the other end.

"The nurse will be right with you," she said and gestured to the waiting room full of people—many too sick to be there—and nowhere to sit. She surveyed the room again and then a hand touched her shoulder.

"Are you here to see Alice Sampson?" A nurse stood before her in scrubs with a stethoscope hung around her neck. She didn't appear much older than Erin with her blond hair swept back into a French braid. Her kind eyes said they had done this before. Take care of the patient and then the patient's family.

"Yes. I'm her daughter." Just saying the words brought tears to Erin's eyes and she suddenly felt so tired she could barely stand. Her mother had never been sick. Erin hardly remembered a day when her mother stayed home from work. She worked hard and showed loyalty to her shop and its customers. Alice Sampson was a rock for all those around her.

"We've admitted her, and I'll take you up to see her. She is infectious, so you'll need to wear a gown and mask. Your dad is with her now."

"He's not my dad. He's her boyfriend."

"I'm sorry."

"No that's fine. I'm glad someone found her. I haven't been around much lately." The tears threatened to fall again.

They walked to the door of her mother's room and the nurse gave Erin a gown and mask to put on over her clothes. The nurse used the waterless hand soap just inside the room and Erin followed her example, then donned gloves. The light in the room gloomy, the only sound was a steady beep of equipment. Her mother lay asleep in the bed with IV poles hanging over her and a tube going in her hand. Brent stood on the other side of the room dressed like Erin and the nurse. He'd stayed with her.

"The tests came back positive for viral pneumonia. She will be isolated from the other patients and have breathing treatments. She is being given IV antibiotics and antiviral meds. We found her dehydrated probably from the fever, so she is being given fluids too. Do you know, does she have a DNR?"

"A what?" Erin stared at the tiny form that slept under the blanket. Could that be her mother?

"A Do Not Resuscitate Order."

Erin shook her head.

"No?" The nurse considered Erin.

"I don't know. Not that I know of. We never discussed it."

"Well, only one of you can stay the night. If you need a recliner, I will have one brought in."

That did it. The waterfall began, and Erin could not stop it this time. Her mother could not leave her. Not like Dad did. This wasn't happening.

"It's okay, honey. They're going to fix her up just fine." Brent had his arm around her shoulder and Erin caved into his chest shaking uncontrollably. He folded her into his arms and shushed her quietly like she remembered her father doing when she fell off her bicycle and scraped her knee. What if Mom didn't wake up? And then she thought of Aunt Toni who needed to know about her sister. She had to call her. She had to pull herself together enough to at least let Aunt Toni know.

## Chapter 32

Bernadette drove to the sandwich shop. It closed at 9:00 on weekdays and she arrived at about 8:30. She would still have time for something to eat before they closed the grill. Then she and Steve could have a little time together. She had no idea where Erin and Rob were. It seemed the four of them were going separate ways a lot these days.

"Hi pretty lady." Steve walked to the counter with a rag in his hands wiping the glass top. "What's it gonna' be tonight? The usual?"

"Yeah, the usual." She leaned over the counter and looked both ways. No one noticed them. She kissed him quickly and then stood back up. "All that and a bag of chips too." She smiled at the boy she grew up with. She remembered the little boy in grade school who she detested, and the man he had become. He was half of their loving relationship over the last two years. She walked to her normal table the four of them shared many times and sat down.

Steve quickly brought the sandwich and sat it in front of her. "I didn't know if you really wanted chips or you were just talking about me." He winked.

"Yep," she said winking back. "And no friends tonight. Just you and me."

"That's okay. I saw Rob earlier. He said he and Erin were fighting. He left with someone."

"What do you mean he left with someone? Who?"

"I don't know, short, blond, big boobs. She's been in here before."

"He is out with a girl? Someone besides Erin?"

"Like I said, they're fighting."

"I don't believe it. She needs to pull her head out and look around her for a minute. She is going to ruin this relationship. And then there's him. The first time they have a fight, he immediately runs off with someone else! I think I know who you are talking about. There were some girls at the library flirting with him tonight." Bernadette took the napkin from the basket and placed it on the table.

"I don't know who she was, but I've seen her in here before. I'll be done soon." Steve walked to the back, leaving Bernadette to eat her sandwich. He began to close the shop.

Bernadette's phone rang, and she glanced at it. The screen read Erin. She really didn't want to deal with this now. Erin needed to talk to her boyfriend and patch things up. She clicked ignore and went back to the sandwich in front of her.

"Okay studying in your room?" Steve hung up his apron and walked Bernadette to the door.

"Yep, I'll beat you there."

Bernadette, the last customer of the night, walked to the door. He kissed her on the cheek as she nodded. Then he turned the open sign around, locked the door and walked to the back where he parked his car, turning out lights as he went.

She walked to her car fishing the keys from her purse. The Jeep sat at the end of the row in the dark. She vaguely noticed a car running with fogged-up windows as she walked past it. Opening her door, suddenly someone grabbed her, and a smelly rag covered her nose and mouth. She struggled unsuccessfully to get away. It was the last thing she remembered.

\*\*\*\*

Toni shoved her way through the door of the hospital room like she came into a courtroom. In charge. She tied the mask over here face and glanced at Alice, then Erin in the corner, and then back to Alice. Erin ran to her crying and they both broke into tears. Alice always took care of them. She played a double roll as mother and big sister. Now she lay in a hospital bed.

"Do they know what is wrong? I mean this is not a cold." Toni wiped her eyes with a gloved hand.

"They said viral pneumonia and infectious. That's why the gowns and masks. They don't want it to spread to anyone else."

"Especially their precious hospital. I hope they are as careful with the patient as they are about the gowns."

"They've been really good to her so far, Aunt Toni. Someone is in and out constantly checking on her."

"Well, they almost wouldn't let me through. They said one person at a time. I informed them I oversaw the underage daughter with the incapacitated mother."

"I'm not underage anymore, Aunt Toni."

"Well, they don't know that."

Erin pulled her phone from her pocket and once again tried to call Rob. He didn't pick up. Then she tried Bernadette again. Probably with Steve. Sometimes she didn't pick up when they had time alone.

Toni stood next to the bed with her hand on the

sister she always depended upon. Everyone did. "Where's Brent?"

"He left so I could stay. He had Mom's phone and called me. He planned to take her dinner or something and he found her sick. She got up to answer the door and almost passed out. We all thought it a cold. But he brought her here and I'm glad he did."

"He's a good man. I'm glad she's found a good man again." Toni idly stroked her sister's hand. Glancing up she saw tears glistened in Erin eyes. "I didn't mean she found a substitute for your dad, you know, don't you, honey? Just he is good to her, and I'm glad."

"Me too. I'm glad too. Oh, Aunt Toni! What am I going to do? I can't lose another parent!" Erin broke into sobs and her aunt wrapped her arms around her.

"You're not going to lose her sweetheart. They're taking good care of her. You said so yourself. And you won't be alone, you have me. Or we have each other. Or something." Erin continued to sob which turned into wracking gasps and Toni held her close then walked her to the recliner to sit down. With only one chair in the small room, Toni sat down first and pulled Erin into her lap. Erin, taller than her aunt, still curled up in a fetal position and Toni pulled her closer stroking her hair.

The door opened again and a head full of white hair poked through the opening.

"Sir, you can't go in there. Sir! At least put this on." The nurse chased Cronkite into the room and pulled his arms into the gown and tied a mask over his face. He quickly pulled it down, so he could talk.

Erin raised her head and sat drying her tears.

"How are you doing, little girl?" He walked to the

chair and helped Erin to her feet. He patted her shoulder.

"I'm okay. Aunt Toni is here."

"Well, we are going to see to it that your mother gets the best care possible. If you need anything—and I mean anything—you call me, okay?" The old man's eye's glistened with tears. "Anything," he repeated.

"Yes, sir." Erin nodded wiping her eyes on the back of her hand.

Toni walked from the room stating she would give them some privacy. Then quickly returned with an orderly in tow. He had a second recliner and tried to decide where to put it. The nurse followed, and they moved Alice's bed and set the second recliner in another corner of the room. She brought more pillows and blankets and piled them up on the recliners; then took the patient's vitals entering the information into the computer.

They all stood in the middle of the room staring down at the woman who lay sleeping with an IV sticking out of her hand.

"She's a lovely woman, your mother. I can see the family resemblance." Cronkite stood on one side of Erin and Toni on the other. Erin nodded. "A blond, red-head, and brunette all in one family. It's a wonder the men aren't standing in line." Cronkite smiled and once again patted Erin's shoulder. "Anything," he said once again.

"Well, how about some peace and quiet?" Alice's eyelids fluttered open. They remained open half-way like they were about to close again. "Erin? Why aren't you at school?" Alice spoke like a mother and viewed the faces in front of her.

A giant sigh of relief escaped Toni's mouth and she smiled.

"It's nighttime Mom. No classes at night." Erin sniffed and leaned down kissing her mother's cheek. "Welcome back."

"It is about time. We were beginning to worry about you." Toni leaned down and patted Alice's head. "How are you feeling?"

"Kinda tired. I slept well for a while, until you guys woke me up." Alice smiled.

"Sorry Mom, we'll be quiet."

Alice glanced at Cronkite. "Are you my doctor?"

"No Mom, this is Mr. Cronkite, my boss. He came down to check on things."

"Nice to meet you Mr. Cronkite. I've heard so much about you. Does everyone know I'm in the hospital? And who is going to take over the shop? Where's Brent, by the way?"

"Mrs. Sampson, you really do not need to be talking. Try to get some rest. The rest of you need to be quiet or leave." The nurse stood observing the three of them, a stern look of insistence on her face. "The doctor would not like all these people in here."

Ignoring the nurse, Cronkite spoke. "Nice to meet you too Alice. I'll be leaving now. I just checked on my two favorite women, and I see they are in good hands. I don't want to see either one of them in the office for a few days. They have other things to worry about." Robert Cronkite smiled and patted Alice's hand before he turned to leave.

"Thanks, Bobby, I'll be in touch." Toni walked him out the door leaving Erin with her mother.

"Brent went home so I could stay with you. They

said only one person at a time in the room with you. But you know Aunt Toni…"

Alice smiled a sleepy smile and her eyes closed. "Okay, get some sleep, hon." Then sleep overtook her again.

Erin punched the new entry in her phone and called Brent to tell him the news, that Mom woke up and talked. Once again, she tried to call Bernadette and Rob before she curled up in the recliner with the blanket over her. She drifted off into fitful sleep.

Chapter 33

Erin woke with a start when the nurse turned on the light over her mother's bed. Barely daylight outside, it must have been shift change for the staff. Her mom continued to sleep through the taking of vitals. Stretching, Erin noticed Aunt Toni's recliner empty. Maybe she went to the bathroom.

She still had not talked to Rob or Bernadette. It was too early to call, but they could read a text when they got up. Surely, they weren't still mad at her. She wanted to be certain they knew about her mother. She grabbed her phone on the window sill beside the recliner and sent a message just as the door opened and Aunt Toni walked in wearing blue jeans with a bag in her hand.

"I wondered if you were up. I brought you a change of clothes and some bagels from downstairs. There is coffee and tea on the cart in the waiting room if you want some. You can use your mom's shower, since I doubt she will be using it, and I even brought you a toothbrush." Toni sat the bag at the foot of Erin's recliner and the bagels on the hospital tray. "Coffee or tea?"

"I don't care." Erin yawned again. "You are a miracle worker, Aunt Toni. When did you get up?"

"The real question is when did I sleep? That recliner tried to kill me all night long, so I just decided to go home and shower, get you some clothes, and come back."

"Like I said, miracle worker." Erin stood with her hands to her lower back and stretched once more before walking to the bathroom. When she returned a steaming cup of coffee awaited her.

Toni smiled and walked from the room with her cell phone to her ear, sipping the steaming coffee. She was back quickly shoving the phone in her pocket.

"Who did you talk to at the library last night? You said someone might testify against Newman and file a rape charge? I'm going to contact the DA today and see if we can get this ball rolling again."

"Her name is Shelly Cunningham and she is a student at TU. I have her number in my purse." Erin walked to the purse that sat beside the recliner and pulled out the paper. "Aunt Toni, I don't know what to say. Thank you for taking this seriously and helping Nicole. She has been through enough. The father of her child deserted her, and now Todd. It is a wonder she has anything to do with men. I know the judge's son is crazy about her and so is the judge. She has their support—and her grandmother of course. Nicole is a very strong person. I hope she knows that." Erin sipped the hot liquid, pulling a piece off the bagel.

"Well she has a good friend in you too. And if worse comes too worse, we might have to pull your "attempted rape" charge from the night at the prom, out of our hats. The more evidence we can present to show what type person he has become, the stronger our case will be."

"Oh, I really don't want to testify. He just humiliated me. He did it just because he could." Erin took another bite of bagel.

"You don't want to talk about it? What about these other girls? What happened to them is much worse and they are possibly going to have to testify to details in open court. Erin Elaine, what happened to you is small potatoes compared to what happened to them, but your testimony could help them out. You are going to have to pull up your big girl panties and get involved if this charge is going to stick. We are going to need all the help we can get." Toni's eyes blazed like Erin had seen in the courtroom.

Aunt Toni hadn't called her "Erin Elaine" in a long time, maybe never. Her mother called her that when she got in trouble. She'd made her aunt mad.

"I'm sorry, Aunt Toni. I'll testify if it helps. And you're right, what happened to me is nothing compared to the other girls"

"It also helps to make you a better lawyer if you have been in the client's shoes once or twice. See if you can get in touch with Ms. Cunningham today and I'll talk to the DA again. I might have to push the Tulsa County DA a little, if necessary."

Erin's phone buzzed with a text message. "Call me" it said. From Rob. She finished her bagel and walked into the waiting room to call him back. There might be an argument and she didn't want to wake her mother.

"Hi. The text said to call you. Are you still mad at me about last night?" Erin stood in the waiting room, with her phone to her ear.

Rob sighed and then he said, "We'll talk about last night later. We have a problem. Bernadette didn't come home last night."

"Well, she is probably with Steve."

"No, Steve is the one that reported her missing."

"What? She left the library about the time I went outside to talk to Aunt Toni on the phone. And by the way, I ran into Todd again."

"Steve is a basket case. Bernadette came to the sandwich shop and ate like most Wednesdays. They were going to her dorm room to study, but she never showed. Her Jeep is still at the sandwich shop. Something must have happened in the parking lot."

"Has he called the police?" Erin began to pace the small room.

"Yes, but they say college girls run off all the time and the fact that the Jeep is still in the parking lot—well, they think she will be back."

"Oh God. Bernadette would not just run off. Something has happened. By the way, Mom is in the hospital with viral pneumonia and is contagious. You can't come up here and I can't leave the hospital right now. Have you talked to Bernadette's parents?"

"Your mom is sick?"

"Yeah, I tried to call you."

"I've been with Steve all night. Steve called them, and Bernadette's dad is about to kill somebody if they don't get busy finding her." Rob's voice sounded tired.

"He should be mad. Bernadette wouldn't just run off. She got ticked off at me about my job last night. But she still went to see Steve."

"Yeah, something's not right. What were you saying about Newman?"

"I ran into him last night outside the library, again. I think he overheard at least a part of my conversation with Aunt Toni because he threatened me. He must have heard me talk about Mom being sick because he said it was a shame about my mom, and if I didn't stay out of his business, someone would get hurt. You don't think he would hurt Bernadette, do you? To get back at me?" Erin paced the room like a caged animal. She had to stay for her mom, but she wanted to go search for her friend.

"I think he is capable of anything. I'll tell the police what you said and maybe that will light a fire under them." Steve yawned into the phone.

"Aunt Toni will talk to the DA again today about reinstating the charges against Todd. I hadn't told her about the conversation we had last night outside the library. I had bigger things to worry about with Mom. I'll catch her up on the Bernadette story."

"Is your mom going to be okay?" Erin could hear the concern in Rob's voice.

"Well, she talked to us last night, but she is sleeping this morning. But they seem to think they can get her through it. Rob, it is killing me that I can't leave here. Please keep me informed."

"I will." He clicked off and Erin paced the room one more time before returning to her mother. When she opened the door, the nurse stood holding a gown and mask.

"You were looking for these?" she asked pulling Erin's arms through the gown and tying her mask over her face in hurry so that it hung at an angle. Her mother sat up in bed eating breakfast.

"Hi sweetie. Have you eaten? I have much more than I can possibly eat."

"Don't eat from her plate," the nurse spoke quietly and then left.

"Mom. I'm so glad you are awake. How do you feel?" Erin walked to her mother's side.

"Tired. Probably because I've done nothing but lay here."

"I worried about you so much." The tears welled up in Erin's eyes again. She wanted nothing but to curl up with her mother in the bed and hug her but knew she couldn't. She had to be strong. She wasn't a little girl anymore.

"Oh, sweetie. I'm going to be fine. The doctor says I probably picked this up from a customer or something. It just hit so fast, I thought I had a cold."

"It must have hit quickly. You were fine on the phone. I really can't remember when we talked last. I've been a little tied up with my job. I have made more than one person mad because I stretched myself too thin lately."

"You love your job. That is a good thing. Anyway, Aunt Toni is here, and Brent has been around a lot."

"And he will continue to be around." Brent walked in the door with a box of doughnuts in his hands. "I didn't know if you felt like eating but I brought these anyway. Erin and Toni might be hungry."

Alice smiled at the man in the mask. "Or Brent might be hungry," she said.

As fast as the door closed it flew open again. A bunch of balloons entered the door followed by Felicity—blue hair the color of the week. She ran to the bed squealing and the nurse chasing her with a gown.

"You have to put this on! This room is infectious and there are too many people in here. The patient needs her rest."

Erin took the balloons from Felicity to the other

side of the room. They could float there until the helium ran out. Felicity was going to be a problem. She thought Alice needed her constantly, and she might not leave unless they shackled her.

Felicity cooed and hugged Alice with her mask over her face—until Toni pulled her off. "Okay, Felicity we are going to have to take turns with Alice. She needs her rest. So, you can't be hanging on her. The doctor says she is to have no more than one guest at a time, and there are several more than that here now. Step back." Felicity stood and smoothed her skirt, wiped her eyes, and surveyed the room.

"I'm sorry. I just found out. And you know I worry." A small squeak escaped her mouth.

"Lord, woman, get a grip!" Toni shook her head and moved away.

"That's okay, Felicity, I need to go soon anyway, why don't you stay for a doughnut. Brent brought several. And how about some coffee to go with it?" Erin patted her on the shoulder.

Felicity nodded and sniffed under the mask.

Erin walked out the door and came back with a container of coffee cups. With all her mom's visitors, now would be a good time to get away for a while and help find Bernadette.

## Chapter 34

Bo Mitchell once more paced the floor in his tiny office. Walking back and forth was limited in the small enclosure. But it still helped him think. He had to do something about the Newman kid before he harmed someone else. It was his duty. He couldn't let the attorney that the Newman's brought in from out of town push his buttons. He had to find a way to shove back. He talked to their local attorney, Nathan Williams, and knew Todd's dad had enough money to make this go away. At least for now. But in Mitchell's experience once a rapist, always a rapist. He would do it again—they always did. But how many women would get hurt before Todd was put away?

He had no idea why the kid thought he had to rape the girls he met. He had the looks and the money to get girls the old-fashioned way. He obviously got his kicks by raping, and he wasn't going to quit. Soon someone else would come forward with another complaint and then he had to bring charges.

He continued to pace as the receptionist buzzed him. "Antoinette Stone of Cronkite and Associates is on the phone."

He had been expecting this call. He cleared his throat and picked up the phone. "Toni, how is your day going?"

"Not so good, Bo. I need to talk to you about the

Todd Newman case."

"There is no Todd Newman case." Bo had to at least pretend he thought he had done the right thing by dropping the charges.

"I know that. The charges were dropped. But I am here to give you some information, so we can get them reinstated. By the way, how's your son?"

Did she know about the donation to the cancer research center? Sweat broke out on his brow. "He's doing well. Thanks for asking."

"That's good. How old is he now?"

"He's five and in school and he is doing great."

"Well, that's wonderful. Bo, I called about the potential Todd Newman case. I have another girl who has agreed to testify that he forced himself on her. Her name is Shelly Cunningham and she talked to my niece, Erin, about the situation that happened last fall. I also would like to add Erin's name to the list of attempted rape victims. We have several witnesses to that one. It took place in full view of the entire senior class of Mannford and some teachers at the senior prom. If her testimony will help get this thing back on the books, she will also bring charges. She hadn't filed charges until now because she didn't want the courts to think the charge frivolous. But considering all the other girls coming forward—not that these young ladies are girls, they're in college now—so considering these women coming forward currently, I think it bears checking into again."

"Toni, these girls, I mean women, what took them so long to come forward? I hope they don't just see a family with a lot of money that they could cash in on."

"These are not civil charges, Bo, we are talking

about criminal charges. Not that a civil suit might not follow, but money is not what's at stake here. What is important is getting a rapist off the streets so no one else gets hurt. Todd Newman is a rapist and he won't quit until we make him." Toni took a deep breath on the other end of the phone.

"Alleged rapist. He hasn't been convicted of anything." Bo spun around in his chair stretching out the cord on his phone as far as it would go.

"And these women are accusing him of rape and attempted rape." Toni sounded exasperated on the other end of the line. Bo had not heard about Toni's niece until now.

"Well until the new women come in and complain, we can't file new charges, you know that, Toni."

"Of course. They will be in. This is just a courtesy call to let you know. I didn't want to blindside you. I thought you had the right to know it was coming." Toni sighed.

"I appreciate that. Is your niece the one going to school at TU who is a friend of Judge Hardridge's bailiff?"

"Yes, she is working part time for us at the law firm while she attends classes at TU. She is in pre-law."

"Keeping it in the family, I see." Bo chuckled.

"Yes, and she's going to make a great lawyer. She's brilliant, and she can be tough when she needs to be."

"Kind of like her aunt. By the way, how is your sister? She's been in the hospital, right? Is that Erin's mother?"

"Boy, you know all the dirt, don't you? Yes, Alice is Erin's mother and she is doing better. She has viral pneumonia and I will be in and out of the office for the next few days helping her. If you need me, my office can transfer you to my cell."

"Okay. Thanks for the call and I look forward to hearing from the other women about this problem." He hung up the phone and stared off into space. Bo knew now he would have to reinstate the charges no matter what Newman's highly-paid defense attorney dug up.

He was the Tulsa County District Attorney and his job was to get the rapist off the streets. He would not be pushed around by an out of town attorney. Let him do his worst.

Chapter 35

Robert Cronkite's phone buzzed. Knee deep in a brief he hoped to finish today, he didn't need interruptions.

"Mr. Cronkite, Sally Elkman is on the phone," Stephanie crooned in her receptionist voice. He immediately wondered what kind of trouble Sally had gotten into this time.

"Bob, this is Sally." Her father always called him Bobby. He didn't expect her to call him Mr. Cronkite, but Bob seemed a little informal under the circumstances.

"Hello Sally. I hope you are not in trouble again." Maybe too harsh. He couldn't expect her to remain the little girl who sat on his lap as a preschooler.

"No. Or maybe yes. I wanted to come down there and talk to you in person if you have time. I've been discussing a situation with the therapist on campus and she thinks I should come forward with some information."

"Information on what?" Cronkite glanced at the screen with his partial brief still unfinished.

"Todd Newman had a rape charge against him."

"Yes, I think those charges have been dropped." Cronkite really needed to get back on the brief and didn't like the interruption.

"Well, I want to… I don't know how this is done.

Can I come to your office and talk to you in person? I have something for you to see."

"Sure, come on down. I'm free this afternoon." Cronkite examined his calendar and the cancelled hearing previously scheduled for the afternoon. He felt relieved to have a little free time to catch up on some things. And now more drama from Sally. He hoped this wouldn't take long. He buzzed Stephanie after hanging up to tell her to send Sally to his office when she arrived. It was a shame about Stephanie. She was a good receptionist, but he had to let her, and Nathan, go soon. After the laptop mess and the visit to his office in the middle of the night, he could not allow them to stay. He waited for just the right time and maybe that time would be coming sooner rather than later. He had plenty of evidence as to what they did on his desk. He waited to see if he could pin the theft of the laptop on them as well. But one way or another, they had to go. He couldn't allow that type of behavior in a law firm he built from the ground up. Having sex in the office after hours was one thing but doing it on the boss's desk— nothing short of contempt.

"I wanted to talk to you about Todd Newman," Sally said when she stepped into his office. She'd arrived much more quickly than he imagined. She must have been out in the parking lot when she called. He still had not finished the brief due next week. He hoped this wouldn't take long. She sat before him appearing more like the little girl he remembered. She had no make-up on and her hair pulled up in a clip. She wore a sweatshirt several times too big. The fashionista was gone. Nothing screamed 'look at me,' like normal. Where were the stiletto heels and eye makeup? Maybe she really did have a problem.

"That's what you said on the phone. Do you know something about Todd that you want to share?"

"I've been dating him off and on since high school." She squirmed in the chair. "I thought him cute and rich and just everything I ever wanted. Well, at least that's what I thought. I was willing to put up with it at first. I guessed he just liked it rough, but it got worse all the time. This is hard to talk about to you. But..." Sally reached into her purse and pulled out pictures she had taken of her stomach and shoulders after Todd beat her. She handed them to Cronkite. "He did this to me and he raped me repeatedly. I want to file charges." Tears welled up in her eyes and spilled down her cheeks.

Cronkite stared at the pictures handed to him across the desk. The purple bruises were impossible to refute, and he could see enough of Sally to know the photo was of her. The injuries, substantial, could not be denied. Robert Cronkite had no daughters of his own. One son—all grown up—he talked to on holidays, but they had little in common. His mother took him and left when he was little saying she could not live with a man who loved his work more than his family. He loved his son but work just got in the way. He missed too many T-ball games and dinners and finally the boy's mother could not take being alone all the time. Cronkite took the blame. Having a daughter would have been worse, not because she was a girl, but because Cronkite dealt with the world at its worst. And most of the time, women got the short end of the stick. Sally would never be his daughter, but that bastard had beaten the little girl who used to sit on his lap and kiss him good night when her mother told her to go to bed. Not just beaten, but raped. Now he knew why Sally changed from the sweet little girl he knew. And then and there his heart broke in two. Not an easy thing to do to a man who had seen so much. He laid the pictures on the desk, so she would not see his hands shake.

"When did this happen?" he asked in a fatherly way.

"I dated him off and on since high school."

"I meant the beating. Did it happen more than once?" Cronkite pointed to the pictures before him.

"Normally, I protested when he wanted rough sex but then I gave in. Last month while we were out, he was in a bad mood. And when I said no—he beat me. He'd never done that before." Sally twisted the tissue in her hands until it broke.

Cronkite took a deep breath. "Okay, are you prepared to bring charges? You will be asked some very pointed questions in open court in front of Newman and his family, not to mention total strangers. DAs don't like to bring rape charges against a former boyfriend. You must know that in advance. But considering the other charges against him, he probably will this time. But, your life will be laid out for everyone to see and the defense attorney will try to make you out to be a whore. That is his job. He is paid a lot of money to make poor little Todd appear the victim here and he will do it. This will not be easy."

Sally sniffed. "I know."

"No, you don't. Not yet. But you will." Cronkite sighed. "However, I will be there by your side the whole time and so will the DA. We will do our best for you. But you will have to be strong."

"I don't have any money…"

"I'm not asking for money. Let's see where this goes and then maybe you can help around the office again. You did a pretty good job last time with Erin."

"Erin hates me." Sally raised her head and reminded him of the little girl again.

"I doubt that. Erin has been working on this case too. She became friends with one of the victims and supports her. She found some others that Todd hurt and convinced them to come forward, too. Why don't you let me make a call to the DA's office and let's get this ball rolling? And, Sally, for what it's worth, I'm so very sorry for what you have gone through."

She nodded and sniffed reaching for another tissue.

"Thank you, Bobby."

He smiled when she called him Bobby.

Chapter 36

The door to Todd's dorm room flew open, and he sat up on his bed, reminded of when he used to live at home with his dad. Not Dad, but Paul.

"Hey bro!"

"Oh, just come right on in. I might have had company or something."

"You do. Your big brother has come to visit."

"Oh, lucky me." Todd loved his brother, but like most big brothers he could be a pain at times.

"I haven't seen much of you lately. Just thought I'd drop by. Thought maybe we could grab a burger or something."

Todd stretched and yawned then stared at his brother. "I guess we could. I'm studying with my eyelids closed anyway. This shit is so boring." He laid the book aside on the table.

"I know. But you have to get through it, so you can get on down the road."

"That's what I keep telling myself. Anyway, sure a burger sounds good. Anything but cafeteria food."

"I hear that. Makes you miss Lucinda's cooking, doesn't it?"

"No kidding. I got tired of her food when I lived at home, but now I'd kill for it."

"Yeah, she's the best. Well, get movin' I'm starving! And this time no running off with the first cute girl you see. I don't want to be left behind again." Paul tossed a jacket he found hanging on the chair at his brother who sat on his bed in sock feet.

"I thought you were too busy with your friends to even notice." Todd pulled on tennis shoes and tied them.

"I noticed that you left. So, did the girl. I told you she dated someone else in the frat house. You dog!"

"Well, she said she needed a change." Todd smiled crookedly at his brother.

"Yeah, I'll bet she did."

"What is that supposed to mean?" Todd glared at his older brother. As kids they always stuck together.

"Well she filed rape charges the next day. I assume they were false."

"Assume? You're my brother and you are supposed to stand behind me."

"I'm behind you. But, they were false, right?" Paul eyed his brother.

"What's with the third degree? Of course, they were false."

"That's what I wanted to hear. Come on let's go!" Paul smacked his brother across the shoulder.

Todd thought for a moment about the girl in the tunnels. He really should check on her. He didn't want her to die—he just wanted Erin to know he was serious. He and her friend needed to understand that he would not be messed with. But his brother didn't visit every day. He came first. The girl could wait.

Chapter 37

They were the three people in the world that probably knew Bernadette best and they needed to find her. She hadn't run off, no matter what the police thought. Erin knew Todd was involved in Bernadette's disappearance after their confrontation outside the library. Not that she could prove it. But maybe the three of them needed to talk to Todd.

"Rob, are you with Steve?" Erin spoke into her cell phone as she left the hospital. She promised to call him as soon as she could get away.

"Yeah, we're at his dorm room now, but about to leave. He wants to check the place we camped last time. He knows she loves it there. Her dad is on his way, so we are waiting on him, but Steve is about to have a cow."

"Okay, I'll be there in a minute. Wait until I get there please."

"Okay. How's your mom?"

"I think she's better. Felicity and Brent were there with her eating donuts when I left. I think they are going to take turns babysitting her today. She needs all the rest she can get."

Erin told Aunt Toni where she would be before leaving the hospital in case she was needed. When she tried to park at the dorm, the lot was full. She finally found a place to park at the far end. Sprinting to the building, she pulled open the door of the dormitory meant for men. It smelled like the inside of a locker room. She imagined the co-ed dorms were cleaner just because of the girls who lived there, but maybe not. Rob and Steve sat in the front waiting area for her when she arrived. Steve, pale and drawn, appeared to have neither showered nor eaten today. They both stood when she walked in and she pulled Steve into an embrace—then Rob. "We're going to find her. I'm sure. She's a fighter. No one is going to keep Bernadette down for long."

Steve sniffed and wiped his eyes, glancing away.

"Right?" Erin prodded.

"Right. So, where is she?" Steve asked as they sat back down.

"I don't know. Let's think this through as if we were Bernadette. Where does she go when she wants to be alone?" Erin tried to think of something to say to sooth everyone's nerves. Especially her own.

"Well, we know she didn't drive, because the Jeep is still in the parking lot." Steve's voice shook with emotion.

"Okay, she is on foot, so she hasn't gone far." The engineer in Rob took over. "What if she walked and fell into a ditch or something. Is there a place near her car that she might have fallen into something?"

Erin went over in her mind the area around the sandwich shop. She remembered the drainage ditch nearby. "Good idea, Rob. What about the drainage ditch or something?"

"Well there is also the Arkansas River, but it is several miles away. And why would she walk when she had a car?" Rob answered. Steve just stared at the wall.

"Something wrong with the car?" Erin grasped at straws. "Has anyone checked it?"

"I think police have it cordoned off because of her disappearance." Steve finally spoke up.

"Are they finally treating this as a crime?" Erin kicked herself for not being in on this situation from the beginning.

"I think her dad finally got someone's attention," Rob said.

Rob pulled a notebook from his backpack. "Okay, the car is still there. Why would she leave it?" He wrote a heading at the top of the page. He charted this out like a problem at school.

"Well, she was mad at me for one thing." Erin felt guilty remembering the last conversation they had about her job.

"Mad at you for what?" Steve suddenly scrutinized her.

"Because I've been spending so much time at work and neglecting my friends. I walked outside to talk to Aunt Toni on the phone and when I returned she'd gone."

"What did Toni want?" Rob still wrote.

"She called to tell me Mom was sick, and I should talk her into going to the doctor. But I started off telling her I found someone else to testify against Todd. Like I said, the job takes a lot of my time recently. After I hung up, Todd burst out of the bushes and threatened me."

Steve gazed at Erin. "What? You hadn't mentioned that until now?" Steve's red face got darker.

"I hadn't talked to you. I went home to check on Mom, and then Brent called, saying he took her to the hospital. I didn't know about Bernadette's disappearance then. I'm sorry. I hadn't told you yet. I kinda told Aunt Toni, but we were talking about Mom and…"

"What did he say, Erin?" Steve appeared more animated. The door burst open and Bernadette's father rushed in.

Ralph Larson resembled his daughter, short with dark curly hair. He surveyed the room and zeroed in on Steve standing by the couch. Steve instantly walked his way.

"Mr. Larson, I don't know what to say," Steve stammered.

"Telling me you have found my daughter would be a good place to start." His face a study in pain.

"I wish I could sir. We were just talking about where to start looking."

Ralph Larson walked over to Erin and put an arm around her shoulders. "I'm sorry, I haven't slept, and I know you kids are as worried as I am. I think the police are beginning to take this seriously. At least I hope they are. How's your mom?" He squeezed Erin's shoulder.

"Better. Thank you," Erin replied.

"When it rains it pours, huh? Bernadette's mother is not capable of much physical activity these days with Lupus. I had to leave her home. But I promised to check in often. Okay, what have you got?" Mr. Larson viewed each of them. Steve nodded to Erin.

"Mr. Larson, I told Steve that Bernadette and I had a little argument at the library last night. Nothing big. I can't imagine her running off because of it. She thought I spent too much time at work and not enough with my friends. Anyway, I went outside to talk to my Aunt

Toni on the phone and after I hung up Todd Newman jumped out of the bushes at me. He must have been listening because he said it was a shame about my mom and to keep my nose out of his business or someone would get hurt. Do you think he could have done something to Bernadette?" Erin glanced at Steve who turned away again. He tried not to cry.

"I don't know but that is as good a place as any to start. I understand that the charges were dropped against him?"

"They were, but several of us are trying to get them reinstated. I guess that is what he meant by staying out of his business. He threatened me. I was too worried about Mom at the time to think much about it." Erin brushed the hair from her face.

The door opened, and Toni walked in flanked by Jimmy, Sara, and Ann from Erin's office. They all had on boots and jeans—even Jimmy. Toni honed-in on Erin and walked directly to her giving her a quick hug.

"Ralph." Toni held out her hand to the missing girl's father. "Erin told me about Bernadette. I called in reinforcements. This is Sara, Ann, and Jimmy; they work with Erin and me. And we're here to help you find your daughter."

Larson's eyes became large as he stared at the total strangers here to help.

"I am talking to the DA about Newman again this morning. Maybe that will assist in bringing charges against him. But for now, I leave you in the capable hands of these three concerned citizens." Toni patted Erin on the shoulder.

Jimmy rolled his neck and cracked his knuckles.

"I have my car," Sara said. "Do you have a plan?"

Erin nodded at Ralph Larson again waiting for instructions as how to start.

Steve spoke up first. "We were talking about beginning at Bernadette's car. If she had car trouble or something maybe she decided to walk and maybe she's injured somewhere. I also wanted to check out the cove we normally hang out at together."

I'll catch up with you later." Toni trotted to her car and headed back downtown.

Ralph Larson nodded. "Okay, let's start with her car." They all filed out and climbed into two vehicles with Larson in the lead.

## Chapter 38

Leaving the cars in the parking lot meant for boaters, Erin led the way down the overgrown path taken many times as children. She thought of Bernadette with her walking stick. She always found one and carried it with her when they hiked and giggled about using it to fight off the spiders and snakes they sometimes found along the way. Tears ran down Erin's face as she thought of her lifelong friend. Tears she could not afford to show to Bernadette's father.

"Watch that stuff, it will suck you down." Erin pointed out the soggy sand where Bernadette almost lost her shoe and the group walked single file down the narrow pathway to the shore of the lake. The bugs were relentless near the water. It seemed impossible to walk through the jungle that tangled around the trees next to the path, but they each kept a look-out for the red T-shirt she had on the last time they saw her. Erin finally stopped when the shore became rocky and impossible to continue without wading out into waist deep water to get around boulders.

"This is where we always came as kids. But we never passed the rocks."

Larson stood staring out into the water, shoulders sagging. He pushed his hat back on his head and wiped his face with his hand.

"She's a good swimmer, sir, and she's smart

around water. She wouldn't go out there alone." Steve stood next to Larson and tentatively touched his shoulder.

Sara and Ann stood back from the crowd wiping the sweat from their faces. The hike turned out to be more physical exercise than both women were used to, but Erin needed their help.

Jimmy had just begun. "You had another plan?" Jimmy who had spoken little all morning stood on the shore and gazed at Bernadette's father.

"I keep thinking of the Arkansas River," Larson said as he surveyed his ragtag band of searchers. "I hate to think of it, but what if she was dumped. Like this cove—no one would think to check there. It's close to Tulsa but far enough away from civilization that she would not be found."

"Any place in particular?" Jimmy rolled his huge shoulders.

Larson shook his head.

"I have a map in the car and we can see where the Arkansas is closest to the downtown area." Jimmy turned taking the path back to the car in the parking lot. The others followed his massive frame.

"Don't forget to watch for the quick sand," Erin called from the back. Now at the end of the line, she knew pulling someone from that mess would not be fun. Today of all days.

"Is that really quick sand?" Ann asked walking back where Erin hiked.

"I don't know. We always called it that when we were kids. It will suck your shoes off and pull you down. But we always found the bottom. I don't know if it really is quicksand or not." Erin walked with the woman she had only seen in the office before today. She appeared tired but determined.

Ann patted Erin on the back. "We're going to find her, just you wait." She smiled a strained motherly smile and they continued up the path.

"Okay, Ralph, Riverside Drive near Peoria might be a good place to search." Jimmy had the map spread on the hood of his car and pointed out the area. "Follow me this time."

Jimmy led the way back to Tulsa. Erin had a sinking feeling they had a lot more area to cover than seven people could handle. And, two of them were already tired.

At the parking lot of the trail head, they divided into two groups and agreed not to wander off the trail. First, they checked to be sure their phones had a signal. Jimmy traveled with Sara, Ann, and Erin; while Larson took the boys.

The hikers trudged on for hours in the weeds and insects for anything red. By mid-afternoon it became obvious the older women could go no farther. They drank the water they brought with them, but no one had eaten. Larson seemed to be going on pure adrenaline. Erin needed to check on her mother, and she called a halt. Jimmy phoned Ralph urging him to meet back at the cars.

"I think we need to talk to this Newman kid." Larson again wiped his face of sweat as he walked back where the cars were parked. "He knows something. I can feel it."

"Ralph, I'm not your attorney but I'm advising you to let that go. Talk to the police, tell them about Erin's confrontation with Todd and what we've accomplished today, then make another plan. But let the police talk to Newman." Jimmy stood by the car as Ann and Sara climbed into the backseat fanning their faces.

"Well, the police aren't doing their job."

"If you confront him, what if he panics and runs? Then where will you be? I mean if he knows something—and that is still a big if—he just might take off. We need to have the element of surprise on our side and the detectives know more than we do about getting him to talk." Erin was surprised at the lawyerly advice coming from the title attorney.

"Mr. Larson, let Jimmy take the ladies home and we go back to the dorm and regroup." Steve, though haggard, still had his head about him. "We can make a new plan from there."

"Okay, you're right. I don't know how to thank you all for what you've done today. Ladies I hope you are not too overly tired. You have been an immense help. I couldn't have done this by myself. Can I buy everyone dinner?" Larson glanced at the women in the car who shook their heads no.

"I need to call Bernadette's mother, she will be frantic by now," Larson said pulling his phone from his pocket.

Chapter 39

When Toni pulled into the office parking lot she saw Howard Newman's Mercedes. "T-Off" the license plate read. Unmistakable no matter where you saw it. He probably met with Nathan. After the conversation with Erin before she left, she felt stressed. Todd Newman thought the law didn't apply to him. He thought with enough threats, and who knew what else, he could do as he pleased. He threatened her niece and he'd tried to intimidate her in the past. He didn't know who he was dealing with. That boy was going down. No, that man. No longer a juvenile, he would be tried as an adult. She collected sworn statements from multiple women that he had beaten, raped, or attempted to rape, if they hadn't managed to escape. Now if he had done something to Bernadette, she might kill him herself. Okay, she wouldn't, but she would see to it he went to prison and got what he deserved. He would find out what rape was all about in the joint. His lifestyle would be severely diminished inside prison. No tee times with the boys and no boating on the weekends. Just hard time.

She burst through Nathan's door in her blue jeans without knocking, red hair flying around her face.

"I want to talk to you." She pointed at Howard Newman as he sat across the desk from Nathan. Both men appeared shocked, unused to being interrupted in mid conference.

"I beg your pardon, Toni, but we are in a meeting and you can't just come barging in here anytime you like." Nathan stood to protect his client.

She ignored him. "Todd Newman threatened my niece—again. Where do you and your family get off thinking that is okay? I am bringing him up on charges for attempted rape the night of Erin's senior prom and that is not the only charge that will be leveled at your son in the next few days." She found herself standing over the man who sat in the chair, her hands on the arm rest and leaning down, getting closer to the older man. He didn't take kindly to people yelling at him, particularly women she thought.

"Now just wait a minute. You can't bring charges. The DA must do that, and he already decided to drop those charges. You'd better go talk to that little niece of yours. She is barking up the wrong tree this time. And I have no idea what you are talking about a prom, but my son graduated several years ago. Those days are long gone." The heavy-set man stood and faced Toni as he spoke.

"The statute of limitations in Oklahoma for rape is twelve years. But he threatened her just last night. Told her to stay out of his business or someone would get hurt. Oh, and coincidently, now her best friend is missing. Any ideas where Bernadette Larson is right now?"

"I have no idea who Bernadette Larson is."

"Well, your son does. And I'll bet he knows something about her disappearance too."

Nathan jumped from around the desk and grabbed Toni by the arm. "Get out. You can't come in here accusing my client. Now get out of my office."

Toni turned and faced Nathan. "The DA is reinstating the charges and a manhunt is underway for Bernadette. He'd better hope that Todd doesn't know anything about her whereabouts or there will be additional charges brought."

Toni turned and left the office. When she reached the hallway, there were several pairs of eyes on her. She'd yelled louder than she planned.

## Chapter 40

Bernadette awoke in the dark room, gasping and blind. She was hungry, thirsty, and desperately needed to pee. She had no idea where she was. She soon found her hands behind her and both hands and feet tied. Then realized she wasn't blind—a blindfold covered her eyes. Her head ached and so did the hip she lay on. Her memories conjured up a hand over her mouth and the sweet sickly smell of the rag that suffocated her. It was her last thought until now.

Something underneath her poked out from the floor and dug into her hip as she lay on the ground. She rolled over off it and onto the other side and bumped into a cool stone wall. It felt rough like concrete and smelled of mold.

She remembered leaving the sandwich shop and walking toward her car just after Steve locked the door. It didn't register until after she passed the midnight blue Alpha Romeo in the parking lot that the windows were steamed up and someone sat inside. By then it was too late. Someone grabbed her and smothered her with the horrible smelling rag, and now she lay tied up on the floor of a dark room. She didn't see the person in the car, but she knew who owned an Alpha—the only one on campus. Had Todd sunk to this? Was he this desperate? It didn't really matter now who did it. What mattered was getting out of there before they came back. She could worry about who later.

Bernadette scooted her legs to the concrete wall with her bound feet, her face already pressed against it. Flipping over to place her back against the wall would not be easy. Normally fit, she felt weak from the rag and whatever she inhaled. She thought science class taught her that ether smelled sweet. It was a liquid that could be turned into a gas. Hospitals once used it as anesthesia. Such facts were stored in her mind for no reason and that knowledge could not help her now. She rolled forward so that her face almost touched the ground, then scooted back against the wall. Maybe she could press against the wall to try to sit up.

Raising her head to pull up to a sitting position, she found her hands underneath her. If she could get them in front, maybe she could get out of this mess. She lay back down and scooted away from the wall again.

Bernadette pulled herself into a ball as tiny as she could manage. Her hands under her butt, she pushed them forward thanking God for the first time in her life that her legs were short. Wriggling like an inch worm she hooked one heel under the rope that held her wrists together. Slowly rolling to the other side, she soon had both heels hooked on the rope. Now if she could pull her feet through. She stretched her body and it resisted the position she'd put it in. She had to relax. She exhaled and once again stretched her arms, much harder this time. Her shoulder popped out of its socket. The pain excruciating, she cried out and instinctively tensed up. Panting in pain she told herself to relax. Which was easier said than done. She needed her shoulders intact to get out of this. The more she strained, the harder this would be. In agonizing pain, she tried to relax, pulling the other foot through the eye of a needle. Slowly and carefully she scooted the foot, and suddenly it slid through—her hands were in front.

Almost free. Her right shoulder screamed when she raised her hands to her face. She had to help the right arm with the left by shoving it up. And suddenly a loud but satisfying pop echoed off the walls. The shoulder slid back in place, but pain radiated down her arm. She lay still panting for a while then she pulled the blindfold off with her other hand and blinked. The room black as night at first, but as her eyes adjusted she saw light filtering down through dust motes in the distance. On the other side of the room, there was an opening.

She felt the knot around her ankles. It held fast as she picked at it breaking nail after nail. She needed a tool. Then she remembered landing on a piece of metal. If it had a sharp edge, it could be her salvation. On her knees she felt around in front of her. It rattled on the floor a minute ago when she sat up. How far could she have moved it? She could begin to see shapes and shadows, but not much else as she felt the floor for the tool she needed. Turning, her toe connected with something and she heard it slide, then hit the wall with a ding.

Bats found their way by sonar, noises bouncing off things in front of them. Bernadette's ears found the piece of metal the same way. Grabbing it like a lifesaver, its sharp edge gouged into her hand. She winced, but a cut would be a small price to pay for freedom. Sitting once more with her feet in front of her she spread her ankles as far as they would go and sliced at the rope with the metal piece. She sawed back and forth across the rope and it began to fray—then suddenly snapped leaving her feet free. She was loose!

Holding on to the metal as a weapon, she stood leaning on her good arm and then stretched. She walked toward the light and quickly stumbled into stairs in the small room. Bernadette used her hands to help her find the way as she navigated the rusty steps. At the top stood a door. Probably locked. She stopped and listened, her ear against it. She heard nothing but the drip of water. Otherwise, there was no sound on the other side. She turned the knob and the door swung out easily into a narrow hallway. She could barely see but leaned against the wall with her good shoulder and walked sliding her hand against it. She had no idea where she was, but she knew she was no longer a prisoner.

The cool concrete walls smelled damp and musty. Several times she thought she saw small pairs of eyes staring at her, then scramble away. Rats lived in sewers and tunnels. It didn't smell like she imagined a sewer would smell, but she had never been in one. Maybe she was in the tunnels that ran under downtown Tulsa. They were dark and went on forever. These weren't the well-maintained tunnels between skyscrapers that business people used to get to and from the buildings and their cars. These were the abandoned tunnels of prohibition legend. There had long been rumors of these tunnels on campus and some of the students bragged about making a game of finding them. But if she got out of here alive, she would never come back for any reason.

She walked forever cradling the sore shoulder and always brushing the wall. She didn't want to stumble away from it too far and get turned around. She did not want to go back where she started or get lost again. She had no idea where the tunnel went, but the wall felt like a security blanket in her mind. Bernadette scraped at the rope that still bound her writs with the metal piece as she walked hoping it would soon fray.

Then the wall stopped, and she ran into a barricade of saw horses and broken concrete. She couldn't climb over them. They went nowhere. Maybe she had gone the wrong way. She stood and studied her surroundings and finally realized she had to turn back. But to where? And she began to panic. What if she never got out of here? She fought the terror that welled up inside her. What if she wandered around in the tunnels until she died?

"Get ahold of yourself," she said out loud trying to calm the fear she felt. Her voice echoed in the dark. If Todd brought her down here, it stood to reason that he didn't carry her too far. She had gone the wrong way when she left the door. If she turned around and walked back the way she came, she would find the door she came out of again and go forward from there. Maybe that would lead her to the entrance. She trembled even more than before, but continued to brush the wall as she walked, this time raking the concrete wall with her bad shoulder. Pain meant proof of life.

She stumbled toward the faint light the opposite way and soon she found the door to her prison again. It wasn't as far away as she originally thought. She hadn't traveled that far after all even though it seemed like miles in the dark. Bernadette took a deep breath and glanced down. The eyes were back. She kicked out at the tiny forms that inched closer to her. They backed away for a moment. They were becoming more and more brave as they checked out the new addition to their home. Well, she was brave too and much larger than them.

She was still hugging the wall with the painful shoulder when—suddenly the wall ended. She felt behind her. The rough concrete stopped at a corner. Before her the hallway seemed bigger. All at once she knew the light shown brighter than before. She moved toward it—and there it was. The sign for "Third Street" painted on a peeling wall—and another door. It must lead somewhere. She stepped back, and taking another deep breath, she shoved the door with her uninjured shoulder.

Miraculously it burst open to a starry night. She breathed the humid air deeply. Freedom never tasted so good. She was in downtown Tulsa as she thought, still dark and no traffic in the street. What time was it? She turned in a circle to get her bearings. In the distance she could see a sign for the gas station she sometimes used. Bernadette was several miles from where she lived—but she was alive, and she could walk.

Todd had been so stupid he didn't even lock the door. Did he really think she would go down that easily? Or was it Todd? She never saw or heard anyone. Yes, she knew it had been Todd. She walked toward the gas station sign. But first she had to find a bush and try to remember how to pee like her mother taught her when they went camping. She was so civilized. With all she had been through, she still had to hide behind a bush to pee.

## Chapter 41

Ralph Larson leaned over the map of Tulsa spread on the coffee table in the foyer of the dorm. He sent the helpers from Toni's law office home long ago. They could do no more in the dark. They promised to be back at first light. He made points on the map of the places they had searched with a black pen. The blue dots were places they might search tomorrow, the red ones, he said they would search as soon as it was daylight. The police thought his little girl not as important as some of their other cases. They would feel differently if their child went missing. Young girls run off—they normally come back, the detective told him.

Steve snorted himself awake and bolted upright. He eyed Larson apologetically.

"How long was I out? Did I miss anything?" Steve glanced around the room getting his bearings.

"Not more than five minutes. Where can we get breakfast?" Larson felt sorry for the boy. He couldn't know where Bernadette was twenty-four hours a day. This wasn't his fault.

"There is a pancake place down the street that is open all the time." Steve rubbed the sleep from his eyes and regarded Rob and Erin curled up together on the couch on the other side of the table. He started to lean over and touch Rob.

"Let them sleep. We can't do much for another

hour anyway. Then we'll get some food and start over. I thought of these places I marked in red." Larson slid the map closer to Steve.

"That part of the Arkansas River is several miles away. I can't imagine her walking that far," Steve said pointing to the map.

"What if she wasn't walking? What if someone picked her up? That would be a good place to dump someone where they wouldn't be seen."

Steve regarded the map. And the tears threatened to start again. He walked to the large picture window and stared off into the distance. The sun would be coming up soon. He saw a hint of pink to the sky. Across the campus the street lights shown down onto the empty sidewalk.

"No one is up this early on a college campus unless they were just getting in from an all-night bender." Steve walked away from the window as Larson walked up beside him.

"You know it is not your fault, right, son?" Larson asked the boy who might love his daughter as much as he did. Steve nodded slightly.

A figure in the distance walked toward the dorm shuffling along with a mild limp, one arm cradling the other. The person viewed the ground and glanced up now and then to see where they were going. Someone stumbled along oblivious of the night, sometimes waving away a bug and then glancing back up at the building. Something about the walker seemed familiar. And then she brushed the hair from her face and glanced up again.

Bernadette!

Steve ran for the door without a word, Ralph

Larson starring after the boy.

"It's her!" Steve shouted and hit the door running. He took the steps two at a time running toward the limping figure. "Bernadette?" he whispered.

The figure ran toward him crying.

"Bernadette!" he shouted this time and ran to her, grabbing her and hugging her to his body. He quickly found himself shoved out of the way by her father who took over—and Bernadette sobbed.

"Daddy. Steve! I was so scared I'd never see either of you again." She hugged them both crying. Ralph Larson wiped the tears from his daughter's face and pulled twigs from her hair and she hugged them both again wincing at the pain in her shoulder.

The door from the dorm burst open and Erin's long legs ran out with Rob right behind her. Erin shoved her way in to the melee and grabbed her best friend wrapping her in her arms.

"Where have you been? We've been so worried!" Erin grabbed her friend by the shoulders. Bernadette winced.

"The abandoned tunnels. When I got lose I was downtown and had a few miles to walk, but I'm here now."

"Was it Newman?" Mr. Larson got straight to the point. He dialed the number of the police station. "Did he hurt you?"

"No, he didn't hurt me. I just woke up and my hands and feet were tied. I got loose and came here. I'm so tired and I hurt all over. Can we sit down?"

Inside Steve's room with the police on the way, Erin took a moment to step outside and call her aunt.

"Aunt Toni, she's here." Her voice broke with

emotion. The emotional floodgates opened when she heard her aunt's voice and tears no longer just threated to fall.

"You found Bernadette?" Toni sounded breathless.

"Yes, she just showed up. She got away and walked all the way home. Todd had her tied up and left to die in the tunnels downtown." The sobs started in earnest.

"You're sure it was Todd? I mean did she see him?"

"No, she woke up alone in the dark and then got herself untied, but she's sure his car was in the parking lot when she was grabbed. She's exhausted and her shoulder is hurt she says from getting out of the ropes. But she seems okay." Erin blew her nose on a dirty tissue from her jeans pocket. "Aunt Toni, I want this bastard caught and I want him to suffer like Bernadette suffered! Talk to the DA. Get it done!" Erin slid down the wall no longer able to stand.

"I'll do my best, honey, and you try to relax. The hard part is over. Bernadette is home and safe. Besides, I've already talked to the DA and a bunch of other people. We've got a case this time and I'm sure they will prosecute. But you keep your mouth shut and don't try to find Todd. The police will handle it from here. If you scare him off, it might be ages before he's found. He has the motive and ability to run."

"I will, Aunt Toni, I promise. And let me know if I can do anything."

"You already have sweetie. Now go take care of your friend."

Erin clicked off and walked back inside the room after drying her eyes.

They forgot about breakfast for a few hours as the police showed up and took Bernadette's statement. They took her clothing, the metal fragment, and rope that had been around her writs that she shoved in her pockets when she got away.

"Guys, I really need a shower," Bernadette pleaded.

Rob ran to the pancake house for takeout breakfast and they all sat in Steve's room eating from Styrofoam plates. Ralph Larson felt reluctant to leave his daughter even when she fell asleep on Steve's bed. He listened to her tell the police what she remembered and seethed at the thought of his daughter in a dark tunnel bound and gagged. Someone would have to pay, but for now he would let her rest and bring her mother back to see her later.

****

Erin pulled Rob up by the hand and tiptoed from the room allowing Bernadette some time to rest. She lay dozing and they could talk later, with only a couple hours sleep, and then breakfast, suddenly exhaustion overtook Erin.

Erin and Rob walked hand in hand to her dorm without speaking, the night finally over. Now they needed sleep.

She opened the door and found the room empty. Erin wondered why her roommate paid rent when she never stayed there. Erin locked the door from the inside. She led Rob to the bed and sat down with his arm around her shoulders. She leaned in to him afraid she might cry again. Instead she glanced up and kissed Rob gently on the lips. Then again. She pulled him down onto her twin-sized bed in the dormitory where she lived since leaving home. She kissed him more urgently and then pulled his T-shirt over his head running her hand down his chest—he sighed. She melted into his body as he drew her near.

"Erin." Rob pulled back staring at the girl in the bed. "Are you sure? This is okay with you?"

"I think it is time. I don't know why I've waited so long." She smiled and drew him near. He unbuttoned her blouse, and shoved back the covers of the bed inviting her in. She felt a longing she couldn't ignore. She couldn't believe she had waited so long. He kissed her neck and slid down her body pulling off her jeans and panties as he went. She reached for the zipper of his jeans sliding it down and then pulled him on top of her. She would never let him go again. He was the most important thing in her life. She wanted to feel like this forever.

She awoke a few hours later in the tiny bed, feeling his naked body against hers and found it warm and comforting.

"Hi," she said sheepishly. She could feel the warmth of a blush.

"Hi back." He smiled and brushed her hair out of her eyes. She snuggled against him, then yawned and stretched staring into his incredibly green eyes and kissed him gently—as her cell phone rang. Bernadette.

Bernadette was alive. Her best friend—next to Rob—alive and well. Todd would pay. There were several people who would see to that.

Rob kissed her cheek as she said hello and he got up, pulling on his pants, then sat back down beside her. They had much to discuss about their new relationship, but Bernadette came first.

## Chapter 42

Cronkite felt judicious. He called the DA, then took Sally to his office to file the complaint. At first Mitchell balked. After all Sally and Todd dated for some time and had sexual relations in the past. The last thing he wanted was a jilted girlfriend bringing charges to get back at her ex. But the pictures of the beating, and the new girl who added her name to the list of people charging rape, slowly changed his mind. He admitted it was time to get this kid off the street and out of society's hair once and for all. But he reminded Sally it wouldn't be an easy trial for anyone, especially the victims. Sometimes the law slanted in the direction of the accused—especially if they had a high-priced attorney from out of town who specialized in getting rapists off. And having money never hurt. But the DA wanted to show the Newmans that the people of Tulsa County would not be messed with. Their daughters were too precious to be left to the devices of a sexual predator, no matter his name or how much money his family had.

And today's meeting with the DA reminded Cronkite why he went into the legal field. He'd made plenty of money as a defense attorney and helped some innocent clients get justice. He also helped many that were not so innocent. But the law said they had a right to defense too, and they got it with Cronkite.

And since he felt judicious, he found it time to take on another problem that raised its ugly head of late. He punched the button on his phone.

"Stephanie, I need to see you in my office please."

The time had come to confront the traitors in his firm. "And call Nathan. I want to see both of you." He knew Nathan sat alone in his office working. He knew what went on in his firm even if it didn't appear that way sometime. He was not the doddering, old fool many thought. Calling them in like this should give them time to sweat a little. Surely, they guessed he knew about the tryst that took place on his desk. Stephanie surely noticed he ordered a new blotter once he found out. The thought of Nathan's naked body disgusted him, and he threw the old one out.

A knock sounded at the door. "Boss?" Nathan stuck his head in. He'd never called Cronkite boss in the length of time he had been there.

"Come in, Nathan, and have a seat."

Stephanie, right behind him with eyes wide, waited to see how this all played out.

"Close the door, will you please? Then have a seat." Cronkite nodded at the woman who took care of his front desk for several years.

"It has come to my attention that the missing laptop, found in the basement near my closed files, belonged to Erin." The people across the desk from him both heaved a sigh of relief. "The same laptop checked out to Erin that disappeared the day her project was moved out of the way for your conference." Cronkite nodded at Nathan.

"Boss, I don't know anything about a laptop—" Nathan began.

"Hush." Cronkite pointed a finger at Nathan. It stopped him short. "You removed it from the conference room that I implicitly provided for her and the case she worked on."

"Well, I had a conference that day and needed the room." Nathan straightened his tie.

"The conference room schedule is held by the receptionist and Stephanie surely knew it to be in use. But be that as it may, I believe that the two of you conspired to steal and hide the laptop in the hopes that Ms. Sampson would not be able to complete the project she worked on."

"Oh, come on, Boss, why would I do that? I know that case has been eating a hole in you for years. I'm glad you finalized it."

"Me too. But nonetheless the laptop disappeared and is now found—low and behold—in my closed files. Hiding in plain sight. That was no accident." Cronkite gazed from Stephanie to Nathan and back again. "It is my opinion that such shenanigans were suggested by Nathan and completed by Stephanie at his bidding. It's obvious that Stephanie would do whatever you want her to do, Nathan." Cronkite could not imagine that the young woman's eyes could get any larger, but they did.

"I don't have to sit here and listen to this. I have work waiting in my office." Nathan started to rise.

"Sit down! I'm not finished. Have the two of you ever noticed the lipstick cam mounted on the eagle statue behind my desk?" Cronkite nodded to the credenza behind him.

Nathan's cool exterior began to crumble. He looked like a kid with his hand in the cookie jar.

"Nathan, I've got to say, the view of your naked

backside is not something I would not want on camera, but I have the DVR recording if you need to see it, I'd be happy to show it to you." The room was completely still and the people across the desk squirmed in their seats. "Stephanie, I thought you had better judgment than that or I wouldn't have allowed you to represent my firm every day. And Nathan." He stopped and shook his head. "Pure contempt on your part. You could have as easily seduced that young woman in your own office, but I guess that didn't give you the thrill of getting one over on the old man. At this moment the movers are boxing up your things under Sara's supervision. You will not be allowed to take anything that belongs to this firm. As far as your clients go, once word gets out about what you did, you probably won't have any. Except Newman, who is as crooked as you. So, get out of my office and good luck with future employment."

Nathan and Stephanie stared first at Cronkite and then each other, neither moving a muscle.

"You are both fired. Get out!" Cronkite yelled and they both ran for the door.

"This isn't over." Nathan turned and glared threateningly at the man who hired him years before.

"Oh, it's over," Cronkite said.

Cronkite leaned back in his chair with his hands behind his head and smiled a vindictive smile.

He still owned this firm.

## Chapter 43

Alice sat on the porch swing in a sweater with the afghan across her lap. Brent brought her a tray with a bowl of chili and a drink. The crisp air sunny and cool, fall was upon them.

"Now you just sit there and let us know if you need anything." Brent winked at her and raised one eyebrow the way he did when he wanted something. He wanted her to rest and not jump up to serve her guests.

Alice, bored now that she felt better, found there wasn't enough to do in the tiny house. Daytime soaps were the worst. She had no idea how people could get hooked on them. She tried not watching them, but she'd seen most of the old movies available on the off-channels too. She could only read for so long before she fell asleep. She wanted to go back to work. But every time she got up to clean the bathroom or do a load of laundry she found herself sitting down again. When would the exhaustion leave her?

She had no idea about a party until Erin came in the back door with Brent behind her carrying a vat of chili. The people she loved most in life brought lawn chairs, ice chests, and food to go with chili. A feast was on.

The air had once again turned cool and leaves began to color. She loved this time of year and longed to go down to the lake to see the trees turn. She might ask Brent to take her. And then he showed up with chili, his kids, and a party.

Felicity brought her new boyfriend—someone much younger than her that matched her energy level. He smiled sweetly when introduced—her arm entwined with his. He was the definition of a boy-toy but they both seemed happy now.

"I brought my world-famous chili," Brent bragged as he carried it in the house.

"He has world-famous chili?" Alice asked Erin.

"Doesn't every man? I mean, that's what he said when he invited us."

Toni came with a date. She introduced him as Tyler Layman, the DA of Logan County. Obviously, they had been dating for a while and were comfortable with each other. This was not a first date. Toni, always secretive about her relationships, often dated someone from out of town. She said her private life was no one's business but hers. Alice could not remember ever being introduced to someone Toni dated. Maybe this time her sister was serious.

Alice had not seen Bernadette since the kidnapping. She shuddered at the thought of the little girl who she helped raise being hurt. Bernadette might have been tiny, but she was also tough when she got out. That attitude alone would help her go far in life. She filed charges immediately against Todd Newman. They found his DNA on the rope she kept stuffed in her pocket after getting loose. Alice hugged Bernadette gently knowing she injured her shoulder, but Bernadette seemed fine. She sat beside Alice on the swing and Brent brought her chili. She had healed quickly.

"So, two counts of rape, two of attempted rape, one

of assault and battery, one of kidnapping, and one of attempted murder? That should put him away for a while." Erin stood in the kitchen with Toni discussing the case out of earshot of the rest of the crowd.

"There will be a party at the country club on Friday night and Todd will be there. Also, a Bar Association dinner that same night, so I'll be there anyway. They plan to arrest him then."

"I want to go. Get me an invitation." Erin's jaw set stiffly at the thought of finally putting a stop to Todd's crimes.

Toni's eyes widened and then she stared appreciatively at the girl in front of her. "I can probably do that. That shouldn't be a problem. I'll be there—and Bobby too."

"I want an invitation for Rob too. He can accompany me, and it will look like a date. We'll dress up. I want to see Todd's face when he is finally caught. It is one thing to bully me at the prom, but quite another to kidnap and leave my best friend for dead—just to get back at me."

"Consider it done, after all this case might never have come together without your help. You have grown up so much, Erin. You have learned a lot in the last three years. I'm very proud of you. You never whined or complained about the job and I know there were tough times. You never mentioned the mess with Nathan and Stephanie—just took it in stride. And then the stolen laptop."

"You knew about Nathan and Stephanie and the laptop?" Erin seemed surprised.

"I know a lot of things. I'm a partner and Bobby and I are close. He showed me the DVR. I think he plans to keep it locked up in case he ever needs it."

"I always wanted to be like you, Aunt Toni. You were always so tough and at the same time elegant. You are a great role model."

"Well, you can do better than me! You are much smarter than that. Case in point that cute hunk you *finally* started seeing as something more than a friend."

Erin smiled. "Rob is great. I always knew that, but when Bernadette disappeared, I guess I realized how much I relied on him."

"Good for you. I'm glad you didn't wait as long as I did."

"Tyler is a nice guy. Are you two serious?"

Tyler walked in the kitchen as if on cue. "Chili?" he said smiling.

"On the stove." Toni leaned over and kissed him handing him the ladle and winked at Erin.

## Chapter 44

The tall dark-haired woman walked in the door of the country club. Her emerald green dress shimmered as she walked, setting off her long chestnut hair. All heads turned to watch her as she moved to the bar. She walked with the confidence of a life well lived and experience beyond her years. No one noticed the men walking several paces behind her in dark suits; all eyes were on her. And there he stood leaning against the bar with a glass of scotch in his hand. He smirked as he studied her up and down and then drained his glass.

"Chardonnay," she said to the bartender. He nodded and smiled.

"Erin," he said walking toward her, "you coming to see me tonight? Great dress." He surveyed her with hungry eyes.

"I knew you would be here, Todd. But I'm not here to see you. I'm here for the party."

"Ah, come on. Don't be like that. Let me buy you a drink."

"Todd Newman," said the man walking up behind them.

"Yeah, not now, guys." He waved them away nonchalantly like insects and continued to stare at Erin.

"You are under arrest for assault and battery and rape in the first degree of Sally Elkman and a list of others, and the kidnapping and attempted murder of

Bernadette Larson." Todd found himself quickly shoved up against the bar with his arms behind him and the cuffs snapped in place.

"What? Sally Elkman, you've got to be kidding." He struggled for just a second and then maintained his cool. A slight ripple of noise ran around the room.

Erin smiled and sipped her drink. "And just about time," she said. "It had to catch up with you eventually, Todd. You can't treat people like a piece of meat all your life without repercussions."

"I don't know what you're talking about."

"Sally told me everything—you know how girls talk. And Bernadette—well, it is a good thing she managed to get loose or there might be a murder charge too. There are others coming out of the woodwork and bringing charges as well."

"I'll be out in an hour, bitch, and I'm comin' for you. You've got nuthin' on me."

"Oh, nothing but a couple of eye witnesses. I can't wait," she said. "Then we'll go to court and you will get what you deserve."

The officers turned Todd around and walked him out the door as he grumbled under his breath. "What are you lookin' at?" he yelled at the older woman who stood in the way. She moved aside. The country club didn't normally see its members arrested on site.

Rob and Toni joined Erin at the bar as they watched Todd escorted from the room he loved so much. The room he had worked many times in the past.

Toni's date put his arm around her as he ordered a drink. The Bar Association had a party tonight and the District Attorney from Logan County accompanied the beautiful redheaded defense attorney.

"You okay?" Rob asked as he kissed Erin on the cheek.

"More than okay." Erin smiled as she took a sip of her wine. "I'm vindicated. He won't be hurting any more women where he is going, and he'll remember me as more than a little girl from high school he messed with."

Aunt Toni smiled. "It has been a pleasure watching you grow up, lady." She nodded at her niece and tipped the glass in her direction.

"Todd's right about one thing, though. You look really good in that dress." Rob took the glass from her hand and set it on the bar. He walked Erin out the door. "You not only look good, you are good. You have done a good thing here today."

Erin smiled at the man she knew she wanted to spend the rest of her life with. It hadn't been discussed, but she knew how she felt now and thought she knew his mind as well. She felt proud of her accomplishment in helping to get Todd off the street. But she knew there were a lot of Todds out there and she had a long way to go. "Thank you."

"I say let's not waste it. I say the good-looking woman and her escort should go out to a nice dinner since they are already dressed up."

Erin smiled. "About that girl you ran off with at the sandwich shop the night Bernadette disappeared..." Erin glanced at Rob out of the corner of her eye.

"Never even kissed her. Didn't want to. All I wanted was you, and I still do." Rob grabbed her hand and kissed it.

Erin's phone rang, and she inspected the screen. Cronkite at the party probably wondered when she would arrive. He wanted to talk business. It could wait until tomorrow, she clicked ignore. She had dinner plans now. She texted Aunt Toni that she and Rob weren't staying for the party—then hooked her arm through Rob's bent elbow and they walked out into the night air.

Todd would be put away where he couldn't hurt anymore women.

## A word about the author...

Peggy Chambers calls Enid, Oklahoma, home. She has been writing for several years and is a multi-genre published author, always working on another. She attended Phillips University, the University of Central Oklahoma, and is a graduate of the University of Oklahoma. She is a member of the Enid Writers' Club and Oklahoma Writers' Federation, Inc. There is always another story weaving itself around in her brain trying to come out. There aren't enough hours in the day!

You can find her at http://peggylchambers.com/ where she writes a weekly blog, like her on Facebook at https://www.facebook.com/BraWars, connect with her on Twitter at #ChambersPeggy, or Instagram at champeggy.